RA Ferrell lives in Raleigh, North Carolina, with her husband and their very spoiled King Charles Cavalier, George. They have three grown children who have fled the nest and moved around the country to have adventures of their own, leaving them empty-nesters and giving RA time to write and travel.

To Cliff, Alexandra and my family. Thank you for always cheering me on.
Christine and Michael – I appreciated all your help and wisdom.

RA Ferrell

CLARITY THROUGH CHAOS

AUSTIN MACAULEY PUBLISHERS™

LONDON * CAMBRIDGE * NEW YORK * SHARJAH

Ordering Information
Quantity sales: Special discounts are available on quantity purchases by corporations, associations, and others. For details, contact the publisher at the address below.

Publisher's Cataloging-in-Publication data
Ferrell, RA
Clarity Through Chaos

ISBN 9781647502195 (Paperback)
ISBN 9781647502201 (Hardback)
ISBN 9781647502218 (ePub e-book)

Library of Congress Control Number: 2021909701

www.austinmacauley.com/us

First Published (2021)
Austin Macauley Publishers LLC
40 Wall Street, 33rd Floor, Suite 3302
New York, NY 10005
USA

mail-usa@austinmacauley.com
+1 (646) 5125767

Chapter 1

Menacing black smoke climbs over my rooftop; flames reach skyward, joining with the smoke that towers over my home; blocking all of the blue. It moves quickly to obliterate the normal view. My pulse and mind are racing. This chaos seems nearby. It closes in on my space, taking over my day. This cannot be happening now.

Not today…

Not here…

Not to me…

I examine the sky, lifting my hand to shade my eyes from the sun. Moms grab their children from the pool; men run to the front of the house through the side yard. Everyone is shouting, protecting their families, and moving together in a race to see what happened on the other side of my home.

I stand alone.

I drop my bottle into the grass, sprinting forward. I jump onto the back patio, running through my home, barely stopping to look where I am going. I bounce off of the wall, not being careful of the furniture or pictures on the wall, trying to get closer to the origin of smoke and flame.

Every ounce of my body is tingling. Nightmare scenarios run through my mind—gas leak, car accident, airplane down, grilling accident with a propane tank or a misfired bomb from Fort Bragg.

I have a bad feeling about this. My stomach drops to my feet.

I run as fast as I can, my sandaled feet slamming into the wood floor. The smacking sound races me to the door. I throw open the front screen, preparing to help a neighbor or someone in an accident in the street. A sharp, burning, acrid odor fills my nose and invades my mouth. It is hard to swallow. I cough and struggle to find air; a chemical smell coating the back of my throat. Something has gone terribly wrong. I automatically reach in my back pocket to grab my iPhone. I know we were going to need emergency services.

With my phone in hand, ready to call 911, I come to a dead stop, immobilized on the front landing. My brain cannot process what I am seeing less than 50 yards away. I raise my hands as if to wipe away the smoke and clear the picture. It appears as if John's Jeep Cherokee is halfway down the driveway and is stuck there. It is hard to tell if it is John's vehicle. I try to squint at the scene, shaking my head like an Etch-a-Sketch, hoping to make it all go away. The manifestation of burning metal is thick and dark. There is a small bowl-shaped black hole in the driveway as if someone has spilled a lot of mysterious dark paint on our clean cement. It is impossible for me to grasp what I am seeing.

Behind the hole is a mostly blue and black mangled metal from the front end of the Jeep where the engine should be. The front of the vehicle seems to be missing and the roof is pulled back as if a giant hand reached inside. Sharp, jagged points are sticking up. It looks like a strange art sculpture, like a modern art scene sitting in my driveway. It's ugly and wrong, but I stare at it, fascinated.

My mind does not understand. My heart is beating out of my chest. I keep wiping at my eyes. I take a few small steps forward, trying to move closer and see better. Glass is sprinkled everywhere. It is shining at me like jagged diamonds across the yard. It catches the light from the flames and distorts my view. The driveway, the Jeep, parts of the front yard…everything seems to be on fire.

Nothing registers as real, although I feel the heat on face. I know the burning is wrong, but I cannot put the scene in front of me into words. My feet are glued to the grass in my front yard. A few of the men are trying to approach the Jeep, but there is too much fire, too many flames grasping out of the sides like hands trying to catch more of my world. Pieces of debris are in the road, in the front yard, in the neighbor's yard. Even some small bits are still falling from the sky—black bits falling in front of me like dirty snow confetti. My heart pounds in my ears, muffling the cackling fire.

Someone has called a fire truck. The firehouse is located at the top of our neighborhood; I always thought having them close by was a nice addition to the area for the Fourth of July parade when they decorate the trucks, or the times they get involved in neighborhood clean-up campaigns. Somehow, I never thought about how close they were for reacting to emergencies. I hear the truck racing down the street, sirens blaring. Neighbors appear spilling out of their houses, staring at the sight from their doorsteps, hugging their children, pointing at my house, at me. I am not moving; I am stuck there. My mind, my heart, cannot register the scene.

John's Jeep Wrangler is on fire at the end of our driveway. My brain finally starts to work. Where are John and Paul? My throat is burning, and my eyes are blurring. Someone is shouting. I am trying to scream for someone to help. The world tilts. Where are John and Paul?

My brain stalls. I reach out towards the Jeep, trying to extract the facts. My throat burns. The hot fire feels close to me now. Jane comes up behind me, takes my hand and tries to pull me back in the house. I cannot move. I will not move back. I need to save my family. I cannot go forward.

Tears are streaming down my face. I hear someone screaming a painful sad noise. All I smell is the smoke; ugly black smoke is filling my lungs. My breathing is harsh, like I have run a marathon. My hand is still holding my phone like a lifeline. John and Paul's picture from moments ago is now staring back at me from the screen. It tumbles to the ground in front of me. What is happening? My mind will not answer the question. I collapse to my knees, sobbing. The ground feels hard and unforgiving.

Where are John and Paul? Would no one answer me? I cannot get any air. I try to catch my breath. I cannot turn away. I stare into the fire and my vision blurs. I try to wipe it away. Everything around me is turning black. Hell has come to my front yard. All around me, neighbors and friends watch as my life melts into the driveway. Jane holds on to me as I cry out for John and Paul. My family, my life; nothing is okay.

Chapter 2

Memorial Day—Monday: Eight Hours Earlier

I need to be loved. The thought floats into my consciousness as I slowly open my eyes in our king-size bed. I'm alone except for the faint sound of the lawn mower running back and forth outside of the bedroom window. The hum of the motor disturbs my rest. John must be outside getting an early start on readying the backyard for our pool party. I reach over and caress his cold pillow. I had been hoping for a different kind of morning.

John is home, not deployed, not away…I sigh.

I had been contemplating so much more for this morning. I mean, I am genuinely feeling the mood. I run my hand down my side, feeling my pink silk nightgown. I picked it to wear to bed last night because it really enhances all my assets. I was sure it would work.

Now, my whole being is focused on the want.

I need this; it has been a while.

For me, the height of anticipation is the moment before—when you know this is going to happen. You are ready, and you can taste your excitement. My eagerness is almost killing me. My mind produces and constructs the foreplay that could have happened.

A hum takes over my body; desire moves though me. It has been a long time since John and I have been together.

I pulse.

I reach over and grab my phone from the nightstand.

Come join me in bed, I text John.

I picture what could have been happening this morning as I listen to the lawnmower move through the backyard.

It is not too late if John comes inside.

I try not to let sadness overtake me as I wait for John's reply. I think about how we have drifted apart this last year. John is finally home, and I am determined to get us back to being us, together, better.

My blank phone stares up at me.

I knew if I could get his attention, the sex would be good this time. I could feel it. I told myself last night, as we fell asleep watching James Bond, that this was coming.

The lawnmower sound moves to the side of the house and away from the bedroom. It is a distant roar now. I wish I knew what I needed to do to get us back on track. I lay me phone back on the nightstand.

John is not coming.

I lie there, and I think back to the last time we were at the beach; my favorite place. If I could convince John to take a vacation, all of our vacations would be a trip to a beach. The sparkling water, the hot sun, the warm air—you breathe differently when you are away from the day-to-day ugliness of life. You can be anyone on vacation. You can be fun; you can drink shots and dance around the pool; you can sleep in late or get up early and catch a sunrise. The stiffness and expectations of life melt away. Smiles and laughter come more easily here; I need more of that in my life. At the beach, a little playful friskiness seems to be on everyone's mind. Hell, isn't that why they created siestas south of the border?

The lawnmower has stopped—John has moved on.

"Goooood Morning, Fayetteville!" blares through my thoughts. "It's 7:45 am in the All-American City, and we are headed into a hot one. Make sure you have your sunscreen and cold drinks ready this holiday as we salute our soldiers. Hey all, do me a favor. If you see a soldier today, give him or her a hug. *Hashtag* sharethelove."

"I am trying to *hashtag* sharethelove," I snap back to the radio.

The announcer sounds exceptionally happy this morning as he babbles on about the heatwave covering the area. Trying to bury my frustration with my husband, laying my head back on the bed with a thump, I raise our new, soft, blue and yellow comforter up to my chin. I deliberately glide down further into the bed, sliding back towards my sexy thoughts. Closing my eyes, I try to picture John and me together, but I cannot. It is no use; the images of us tangled in the sheets are gone. My body is still ready for action, though, and I can feel myself pulsing. I have been robbed. What I thought was going to be a nice leisurely morning with my husband of sixteen years has been interrupted by his need to mow the lawn. I breathe out loudly in frustration. I kick my feet under the covers like a two-year-old in Toys-R-Us who has been refused his favorite toy. I had been so ready for this morning. I take a deep breath, inhaling fabric softener from the comforter and exhaling sadness and frustration.

I remember us falling asleep last night watching the wall-mounted TV that hangs in the corner of our bedroom. James Bond movies are John's favorites; he has seen them a dozen times, but he always wants to watch with no distractions. I open my eyes again and stare at the ceiling. The stark white, boring wall paint mocks me. I am struggling to give in and let go. I want more. There is nothing exciting happening in our bed. I fall back into reality.

Ugh, I hit the comforter with my hand. The bed responds to my anger with a small squeak of its springs like it is laughing at me. Even the bed knows nothing happens here. It is no use. John is gone. He has moved on with his day.

Daylight continues to stream in through the window, beckoning me to rise and join the day. I sigh and sit up, pushing myself forward, away from my sexy thoughts, away from what I crave.

"Mom," my fourteen-year-old son slides into the room. He is getting tall; his arms and legs are stretched out and gangly. Dressed in baseball practice clothes, he is the cutest gumby I have ever seen. I smile at him. My pride knows no bounds.

"Mom, have you seen my Rainbows? Jake is picking me up in five minutes; we are going to head over to the academy and get in some batting practice before the party," the awkward, almost incoherent words come out of his mouth as he stuffs it full of Eggo waffle, no napkin in sight, without a break or a pause. He is all teenage boy—messy hair, no shower, no cares except food and baseball.

I sit on the bed and take him in. A big stupid grin spreads across my face. He really is a good-looking boy.

"Your flip flops are probably under the dining room table where you left them last night after dinner."

"Cool—cooool," he responds with his new catch phrase. The first cool comes out high and fast like he is still a small boy; the second part he tacks on, lowering his voice and keeping it slow, showing he is growing into a man. He is using it as one word to show us where he is and where he is going, and a simple okay is not his style. He smiles back a big, white, toothy grin, turns, and sprints out of the room with a wave of his hand and thumbs up.

"Paul, do not forget to take some sunscreen and a PowerAde with you," I shout after him.

"Yeah, Mom, I got it!" Paul hollers back from across the house.

Paul walks back in with a second waffle, holding his flip-flops.

"Hey, Mom, Jake's parents invited me to go to Boston with them at the end of June to look at colleges. They are making a trip up the east coast. Can I go?" he finishes off the second waffle.

I sit and think for a minute. I do not like the idea of Paul being away from me for a whole week, but I like his friend's family and John is home. Maybe more time alone together will do us some good. I weigh my answer. I hate the idea of Paul liking a college that far away. I could never let him go so far. I like being able to see Paul regularly and be a part of his life.

"Let me think about it. You know I am not thrilled with you going that far away for college," I try not to sound like a helicopter parent.

"Okay, Mom, I get it, cool—cooool. I don't think I would like those schools anyway. It's more of a road trip with my best friend. We could become Instagram famous taking videos. Two dudes on the road; road-dudes," Paul laughs as he heads back to the kitchen. I shake my head at him. Instagram famous is not what this family needs.

I hear his best friend, Jake's, blue Ford pick-up truck pull into the driveway, playing a loud country rock song. The bass is loud, infiltrating and vibrating our house. The chorus echoes through the neighborhood. It's a song for tailgating and line dancing on Friday nights. It is jarring in our quiet *cul-de-sac* on this holiday morning. The catchy refrain is almost obscene; asking the girl to shake her bootie. I am sure it will be stuck in my head all morning.

Paul shouts back, "Bye, Mom," as he heads out the front door. The screen slams closed behind him. I hear Jake's truck back out of the driveway, the song fading away as they head down the street, and quiet descends on the neighborhood.

I turn and examine the lonely cold pillow lying next to me on the bed. John's white pillowcase looks untouched. I reach down and run my fingers gently across the surface. No John here to pull me in for a kiss.

I think back to an anniversary trip we took five years ago to Anguilla in the Caribbean when John could not get enough of me, enough of us together. I wonder what changed. Were we getting older, or was there something more I needed to work on?

His pillow is indifferent to my thoughts. I feel the soft material between my fingers and flash through the images of the steamy dream I had last night. I realize that it is mostly scenes from the Bond movie. With the dichotomy of my reality and my dream sinking in, I sit and wish I knew how to change my marriage's path. John's side of the bed looks like he had not even slept there last night; it is neat and smoothed down, not a ripple or dent from his existence except for the sheet slightly pulled back where he had slipped out. If I didn't know better, I would have thought he was deployed, and I am sleeping alone, again.

But, no, John is here with me in Fayetteville. I should be happy. I force myself to think happy thoughts. This is what everyone waits for in military families, the times when our loved ones are home together. I pick up his pillow and hug it to me. The army was letting us keep John this holiday, perhaps even for the rest of this year. No orders to deploy are on the horizon; however, I know this could change at any time. John had been away more and more the last few years. My life might not be a sexy day at the beach, but my husband *is home* and somewhere close by. *Here* at *home* and *together*, that is something to be thankful for in my heart. I repeat this mantra to myself in a quiet whisper—*Here, home, together*—holding John's pillow.

This is not the time to feel sorry for myself. If I look around, I see that I have more than most. I need to stop this train of thought and count my blessings. I quickly pad down the hall to the master bathroom. I admire the wood floors. They are elegant and polished, the smell, the murphy's oil soap, lingers in the hall. The floors gleam back at me, reflecting my shadow. Everything looks perfect; I am proud of our home. I cleaned the house all weekend getting ready for John's unit to come over for our Memorial Day pool party. As a military family who recently spent a six-month deployment apart, we take this holiday seriously.

I stand there for a moment, thinking about the stress of all of the deployments. I shake my head, trying to loosen the sad and melancholy thoughts. I was not going to dwell on deployments or John being gone, not today. Today, John wants to celebrate with his men, his friends, and that is what we are going to do.

I was given my marching orders a week ago, and I planned to throw the best damn Memorial Day pool party this unit had ever seen. I had been creating lists, cleaning, and making trips around town collecting items all week. As the day approached, I was confident everything was going to turn out great. Because he was a major, John did not usually invite everyone over; he wasn't supposed to. As John's wife, I learned that we do not complain or make waves. I advance forward like a good soldier once given my orders. *My life is fabulous,* I try to tell myself. *I have an abundance of things to be thankful for. I need to keep it all in perspective.*

I inspect my body in the bathroom mirror, noticing I need to tone up and hit the gym. I take a moment and rub my hand down my chest to my stomach and back up across my neck. My skin is not showing wrinkles, but they were coming. I stare at my reflection. My long brown hair is resting on top of my head in a messy pony tail. I am not a Victoria's Secret model, but I look pretty good.

"Ha!" I laugh as I wave my hands in the air over my head, pointing at myself in the mirror, sticking my tongue out like a small child. "You should have known it wasn't going to happen. Today is going to be a busy day," I taunt myself out loud.

I brush my teeth. The mint toothpaste we switched to recently is a little too strong for my taste, but John likes it. I pull a face in the mirror as I finish brushing my teeth. Staring back at me in the mirror, I see a fantastic mom and a good wife who looks good at 36 years old. I stand up straight, talking to the mirror.

"I am me, Stella Ann Finch. I am good enough," I laugh at myself. It sounds like I am on one of those self-help videos you find on YouTube where they try to sell you wrinkle cream or an ab buster. I step back a little from the mirror, taking in my full picture. When I was younger, people would say I looked like Eva Mendes in Hitch.

"I should go to the gym more," I say to myself as I turn to inspect my butt. I could go on Post and work out or join the Health Plex off Skibo Road. Workout, get in better shape, really turn John's head like in the old days. Turning around in a circle, I inspect my body once more and shake my head at myself. I need to let go of the disappointment from this morning.

I rinse off my pink toothbrush and drop it into its slot in the white marbleized cup next to the faucet. The master bathroom is in order. All of the new matching blue towels are hanging perfectly from the towel bars. The room could have been staged for a five-star hotel. I work hard to make our new home look its best. I do a vogue-mode groove with my hands framing my face as I send a kiss to the mirror and strike a pose. Laughing at myself, I head to our newly remodeled and upgraded kitchen to grab a cup of coffee.

As I walk through my home, I start to reflect on John and what made him decide to mow the lawn this morning. We have a lawn care service. Maybe he is having second thoughts about today. I pour my coffee and enjoy my new spotless granite counter tops, running my hand across them like a caress. I love the smooth cool feel. The counters make me smile. I always wanted new fancy counters and upgraded stainless steel appliances. My new kitchen could be an HGTV star. It is perfect. I will be the envy of all the army wives today when they see it. They are going to love it. This is going to be the best Memorial Day party anyone has ever thrown in Fayetteville. Today is going to be memorable.

Chapter 3

Carefully, I step through the perfectly clean, white French doors, making sure I do not trip on the gray metal threshold and spill my coffee. As I move onto our back deck from the dining room, the smell of fresh-cut grass hits me in the face. I am not proud of this, but I am jealous of the newly mowed green grass getting all of John's attention this morning.

I take a sip of my coffee and frown.

When John is home, he always makes the coffee a little too strong, but he likes it that way—strong, black and hot. Scorching hot. It is not a taste I care for, but John is happy and home, and that is what matters.

I like my coffee warm and with lots of sugar-free hazelnut creamer, like a flavored latte. I cradle my favorite, big, blue mug that holds the right amount of coffee, more than a regular coffee cup without being too heavy or too silly looking. I found this set on a recent trip to the South Point Mall in Durham. I thought they would go perfect with the new kitchen. Paul and I had gone there to find him some new shorts and swim trunks because he had outgrown everything from last summer. My boy had grown a foot taller in the last few months. Thinking back, it really had been a fun day of mother—son time. We had joked and laughed the whole time; we had even stopped at the Cheesecake Factory for lunch, ordering sandwiches and three slices of cheesecake since Paul could not decide which one was his favorite. Of course, this was way too much food, but Paul made me practically roll in the aisle with laughter as he finished off every bite making faces like he was a WWE fighter. Pretty soon he will be driving, and girls and then college will pull him away from me. I shake away the worry; we have a few years until he is gone.

I move slowly on quiet bare feet onto our wooden deck, still wearing my pink silk nightgown. Paul will not be back for hours, and it is too hot to put on a robe, or at least that is what I tell myself as I spot John's nicely shaped backside. I know I look good in this nightgown. I picked it out on purpose to wear to bed last night.

Looking out, I see our yard is ready for the day. John did a bunch of work while I slept in. I watch him arranging the grills and tools with methodical precision as if he is cleaning his weapons or preparing for surgery on one of those hospital drama TV shows. John does not turn around as I walk out, but I know he hears me. He has already showered, shaved, and dressed for the day. He even pressed his gray cargo shorts and new stars-and-stripes blue T-shirt I purchased especially for today.

I take a moment to admire John. My husband is a handsome man. Waitresses and other women in customer service always comment when we go out that he looks a lot like Brad Pitt. Like Paul, he is tall—long and lean—but with sandy blonde hair, cut close. He is starting to show the first hints of gray at his temples. This only makes him more handsome and highlights his green eyes. He really has the chiseled man look down. Somehow, he has kept his six pack abs since college. When the movie 300 came out, we joked that he should have applied as an extra. I am a lucky girl; I need to remember to count my blessings. I should appreciate that John got up early and spent all this time working in the yard today. Most wives would kill to get some help around the house.

As I look on, the quiet of the morning is punctuated by small birds trying valiantly to get my attention as they fly, crisscrossing the backyard, perching on the thin branches of the trees. I assess our backyard. It has come together since we moved in. The Dogwood trees are beautiful, growing up and filling out over the last year. The lawn service guys I hired to work on the yard have really paid off in this area. I pat myself on the back for a job well-done. We have a picture-perfect party yard. All of branches full of leaves would bring welcome shade as the day rolled on. I look up to the sky. The sunshine is bright and clear and there is not a single cloud. I like to think of this brilliant sky blue as unique to here—Carolina blue. Life is calm here on this beautiful morning, and I know this party is going to be amazing—everything John had asked for when he came home last week. Fingers crossed that John will be so happy with me good things will follow.

I settle into my patio chair, appreciating the new green and blue flowered chair cushions I had purchased to dress up the patio for the party. John's back is still facing me. I like the new cushions; they are bright, and cheery. John disagreed, saying that they were too flowery. Maybe after the party I would look around for a more geometric pattern. John likes stripes; maybe I could find that online or in Raleigh. Now that he was back home for a bit. I wanted him to be happy. I can picture us using this area a lot this summer for grilling out.

I survey the backyard and notice that John has pulled the dozen white folding chairs out of the garage. I had purchased them for my book club luncheon in April. The pool is spotlessly clean, and he has even brought out the extra, striped beach towels from the downstairs linen closet and placed them on the new square, metal side table nearest the pool stairs. I had tried to think of everything that we might need to make this party a hit.

John must have been up for hours. I should have helped him with all of this. I wonder when he left our bed. John is a can-do type of guy, always doing everything above and beyond. It is one of the reasons I fell in love with him all those years ago. It dawns on me that maybe he is mad because I slept in and that is why he did not answer my text. I tap my phone. The screen lights up, and I have no missed messages or colorful bit emoji responses waiting. I frown looking down, turning the screen back to black.

A stack of colorful pool floats and a few multi-colored beach balls are all inflated and sitting by the pool, waiting to be thrown in. Knowing the families coming today would love those, I picked them up yesterday as I was finishing last minute errands.

I lay my blue coffee cup down on the shiny surface of our glass patio table and notice John's cell phone. As I touch it, it lights up, and I notice that the screen saver is a picture of his Jeep. I raise phone up to get a better look. I don't know why this annoys me; but it does. I go to place his phone back on the table, but it clatters out of my hand, hitting the glass surface. The *bang clack bang* of the phone hitting the table and bouncing makes me jump like a child who has gotten caught stealing candy. I scramble to contain the noise and capture the phone as I realize my last text is no longer waiting to be responded to on his screen. John puts his grill tools down and turns around to face me with a smile on his face.

"Good morning, beautiful!" John says with a wink.

"Missed you this morning," I quietly respond. I decide to get up from my chair and scoot across the deck to give John a kiss. This is my chance to get his attention and let him know I am ready for more whenever he is. John's emotions lately can be very mercurial. He is not paying attention as I approach, and he lifts the grill, moving it right in front as me as I get close. It almost lands on my toes.

"John!" I exclaim loudly as I jump back.

"Oh, sorry, Stella. I was trying to make sure the grill was sitting right. This leg seems a little wobbly on that side. I do not want it to tip over today."

John looks contrite as he explains about the grill. I stand there looking at him. Today is a big day, and I am not sure if I am ready for a conversation on our sex life. I feel like I am opening a can of worms. I look back at my coffee growing cold on the table.

"We have lots to do today. I couldn't sleep. I wanted to get straight to it," John breaks my silent pause with his abrupt words. He is always in a hurry to go to work, always on the move. Sometimes I wonder why he cannot sit down next to me and enjoy all that we have. Lately, I keep trying to make everything perfect, to create the dream home we always wanted, but nothing seems to draw John in. He has not been interested in the remodel updates or new furniture choices. I sit down at the patio table and sigh behind my coffee cup.

"I know, but I still missed you when I woke up," I reply softly as John turns back around to his grills, absorbing himself once more in his task. I am not sure he heard me, maybe I should try again.

My fingers stroke my coffee cup absentmindedly. I sip the last of my coffee.

I try to be the good, understanding wife. It has not been easy for John and me this last year. Plus, I do not want to piss John off today. Even before he left the last time for six months, we were not on track. No time for marriage drama when the army is calling. Then ten days ago, he had returned home more distant than ever. Normally, he did not talk much about what happened when he was gone, but this time he did not want to talk to me about much of anything except this party. I think he is trying to show his higher-ups that he is a good leader and worthy of a promotion. It is my job to help him. I want to shine here today. I need him to really see me.

I sit there thinking of what to say next. I do not want to argue; maybe I should thank him for all his extra effort this morning. I start to clear my throat and gather the words I need to say as John walks away. I am not even sure John heard me; my eyes follow him as he turns and heads into the house onto his next project.

I let out a sigh, slump down in my chair, and play with my long brown hair. It has fallen loose from the messy bun. *That did not go well,* I think to myself. I adjust the straps of my pink nightgown.

"Buck up, buttercup," I say out loud to the birds in the backyard. I need to be happy that John is home. I know I should be happy that I have an amazing son, a wonderful home, and a handsome husband. It is getting harder and harder for me to find that inside myself.

Before I go in, I walk around my backyard, inspecting the items that John has laid out, and I think about my marriage. Sometimes even when he is home, I am sure he is a million miles away somewhere else. I know John has a lot of responsibility; I feel like he carries it all on his shoulders like a rucksack. Projects make my John happy, and today is a big project.

We bought this house almost two years ago when the army moved us here from Kentucky. I worked hard to turn it into our dream home. Before this, we had always lived on post. John did not complain about any of the expense or upgrades to our new home. I look out across our backyard, admiring the Dogwood trees, fresh-cut green grass, in-ground pool, and a profusion of bright pink, purple, and yellow flowers lining the new back fence. I had even added new flower boxes around the deck this week for the party. Standing here in my bare feet and nightgown, it is hard not to enjoy the scene; this is what we had wanted for years as Paul was growing up and we moved from one on-base housing assignment to the next. A lovely home of our own had always been the goal. John and I had talked about this for years. The sight of all this should make me happy, but instead my stomach is a ball of nerves. I stroke my hair and squish my bare feet into the soft grass.

Taking a moment, I look up at the trees lining the fence and covering it in bright green leaves. Each leaf bleeds into the other so that it is impossible to see where one starts and one finishes, like someone had smeared green paint across a canvas, blurring all the lines. I have to look closely to the see the individual leaves through the bright sunlight. Staring at them, I notice the ragged edges of an individual leaf and how one leaf shadows over the others. Not all the leaves are bright green; a few are tinged a darker color. This jagged, darker leaf blends in and is lost in the mass of leaves on the tree. The more I look, the more I see the jagged and hiding leaves. Someone looking from afar would think all the leaves are perfect on trees in my backyard. I like to think my pretty trees are perfect. I try not to look too hard for the flaws. I lower my gaze.

Breathing in the fresh cut grass and feeling its softness beneath my feet, I embrace the smell, stretch my arms above my head, and slowly twirl around in my pink silk nightgown. I take in the loveliness that is my backyard. I repeat to myself that I can make this work. We are going to be happy. I remind myself that all marriages have their ups and downs.

I stop my musing and make a decision. This party is going to be the catalyst that gets my marriage back on track. I can feel it; something is going to happen today.

Chapter 4

A few hours later, our backyard is full of happy families and will be that way most of the day. Our guests started showing up right on time. John would have expected no less from his troops. I am excited to see everything going so well. I feel like there is a little extra pep in my step as the day moves forward.

John put the call out for lunch to be served at noon, and like clockwork the cars started to arrive, lining our street and filling up the neighborhood. Most of the troops have never been to our home before, but John and I welcome them easily into our beautiful house giving everyone a tour of all the updates we have completed. Soon everyone is relaxing around the pool or on the back deck with a cold drink.

I am proud of myself. Our party is a success, and John will be happy. The music playing through the back speakers is a good mix of summer tunes, easy to listen to and fun to sing. I start to hum to myself. I am standing alone on the back corner of the deck of the house, surveying the party to see if I am missing any details. It is a good thing that I stocked up on a ton of hamburgers, hotdogs, rolls, chips, and drinks at the warehouse store yesterday. John was supposed to have gone with me, but at the last minute, he called and said he was tied up at work. That was okay, I handled it. Pushing the big flatbed cart down the aisles was like a mini workout. I few months back, I had been attending kick boxing classes, but I had let them fall away as I got busy with Paul. With John gone all the time, I really try to be there for Paul, attending games and even baseball practices. I want him to know his parents support him. Sometimes I feel like I have been raising Paul all alone for most of his life. John always seems to be gone.

My mind starts to wander back to what I want. *Maybe John will be so happy with the party and how everything went today that I can spark his interest tonight. Sex! Sex, it's all I can think about lately.* I am going crazy.

I am too carried away with these thoughts. I need to focus on John's party where I am going to catch his attention by being the best wife on the planet. Running my hand threw my long brown hair, I straighten my T-shirt to make sure my outfit is in place and plaster a big smile on my face. I walk down onto the lawn and start a conversation with some of our guests about how nice the weather is today. The music is really happy, and everyone is in a good mood.

By midafternoon, John has shown off his skills by grilling dozens of burgers and hot dogs while greeting guests and telling stories about the various places we had been stationed during our marriage. The smell of charcoal burning in the two identical, round, black Weber grills still permeates the backyard. The remains of a few plates of burgers and chips are scattered across the folding tables that are dressed in red, white, and blue tablecloths.

I need to get those plates cleaned up before they attract bugs. No messes, only fun times, runs through my head. I want everyone to be having fun, not swatting at flies. I scurry to take care of the problem before John notices. From my vantage point up by the tables, everything looks patriotic and festive. Hanging across the backyard are patriotic doo dads, flag-colored objects from the party store fluttering in the breeze. A big sheet cake with the American flag frosted on it sits half-eaten in the middle of it all like a forgotten friend. I had already eaten two small pieces of cake this afternoon but cannot resist scooping off a little icing from the side with my finger. The sugar melts in my mouth, but somehow it is not as sweet as I remember from earlier. I turn away from the cake, unhappy with my thoughts.

I hear John across the deck telling a dumb blonde joke to some of his guys. I had heard this joke a hundred times during our marriage; it is not my favorite. Degrading jokes about women get my goat. If it wasn't John telling the joke, I would probably go over and make a comment about his dating life being off, all that swiping right must be going wrong or something to be so down on women. I switch to watching a hand-full of kids playing in the pool with a multi-colored beach ball, swatting it around while splashing water. The children's fun is contiguous. I start to smile. A real smile, maybe my first one all day.

Everyone in the backyard seems to be getting along and enjoying themselves. Laughter can be heard sprinkled throughout the conversations. Today is for family fun; no serious conversations about politics or talk of deployments here. As I clean-up the plates, I overhear the guys of the unit sitting in a circle off to the side. They are talking about the training exercise they were on last month here at Ft. Bragg. They are joking about all the rain we had and how it messed up their timeline. How it filled their boots and made their tents unlivable. One guy is joking about how he was actually wishing they were back in the desert, in the sandbox away from the Shrek size mosquitos that ate them up. They start to laugh and compare bug stories as they drink their beer.

I stop and listen. I am confused by their conversation.

I don't understand their conversation throws me for a loop. *They were all here last month at Ft. Bragg and not in the Middle East with John?* That seems odd. His team is always with him. John was deployed without his team or they came home earlier, and he did not. Maybe I am hearing the guys wrong. I will have to ask John about this later. I continue to clean up and organize the remaining food, wiping away my worrying thoughts. Right now, I need to concentrate on making this party a hit for John.

Bill, a chief warrant officer in the unit, walks up and gives me a big hug. He holds on a little too long and his arms feel a little too tight. I am a shocked by his overly-flirty manner.

"Stella, this is a fantastic party," he croons as he starts to sway to the beach music. "You have really done a bang-up job here. I hope John appreciates you." He is standing very close to me.

"Do you shag?" he asks as he reaches for my hand. I can tell he has had a few beers.

"No, I do not know how," I sputter out as I try to free myself from Bill.

"How did John get so lucky to have such a pretty wife? You are fantastic," he continues.

"Wow, thanks, Bill. I think John is pretty great, too. Where is your wife…Susan?" I try to redirect him, searching for his wife's name in my memory.

"She left me and took the kids back to Missouri," Bill laments while taking a swig of his beer. "I did not cheat or nothing." He tries to swing me into a dance move.

"I didn't know. That is terrible," I say as I move to extricate myself from Bill's arms. I point at the cake.

"Did you try the cake?" I stutter, grasping for anything to distract his hands. "Let me get you a piece." I sit Bill down with a large piece of cake. As I am collecting his fork and napkin, Juan joins us. Juan is new to the unit. I have only met him once before and I am not sure of his rank.

"Hey, can I get a piece of that, pretty lady?" he asks walking up behind me.

"Yes, of course. Why don't you join Bill?" I point to the table behind me.

I am flattered by Juan's compliment. I know they are just words, but it felt sincere. Juan helps me with the plate as I cut his slice of cake.

"Thanks for putting this all together. You did an amazing job today."

"I was happy to do it. You guys have been gone so much," I reply.

Juan looks at me and starts to say something but stops. Instead, he lifts a forkful of cake into his mouth and smiles.

"My girlfriend is trying these new kickboxing classes they have on Post, have you heard about them? They seem to be all the rage," he says, redirecting the conversation.

"Um, yes I have gone to a few of those, though not recently. I stay pretty busy with our son, Paul. I did think they were cool though. I am more of a Zumba girl myself, though." At that moment, another guy, a friend of Juan, comes around the deck with one of the kids' squirt guns. He shoots water at Juan and me while laughing.

"Juan stop eating that cake we have a run in the morning, and I left you in the dust last week. Stop the insanity," he shouts. We all are laughing. It feels good to laugh. I look down. My white American flag T-shirt is soaked through, showing off my new lacy bra.

I glance around the area for John. He is standing with a group of new wives with his back to me. I hear them all laughing at something he has said. A flash of strong emotions rolls over me. It is a wave of want mixed with jealousy and sadness that I cannot hide. I know my reactions are reflected in my face, making me turn away from the group.

Juan and his friend move to eat more cake with Bill at the table. They start a discussion about whether they are going to have fireworks on Ft. Bragg tonight. Bill is sure they only have them for the Fourth of July. I keep looking over at John with the wives. He does not look over once. I do not have much to say about fireworks.

I notice the older boys were running around the house with water guns, but the brightly colored toys are now abandoned on the lawn. Paul and his friends have since moved on to the side of the house to play ping pong. I walk around the yard with a plastic laundry basket to collect the discarded toys before somebody steps on one or a toy water gun falls into the pool filter. I do not want anything to upset the day. I need to throw a fabulous party. I feel like a lot is riding on today.

As I am coming around to the back deck, holding the basket loaded with toys in front of me, John steps out of the house. He has an irritated look on his face.

"We are out of ice. The icemaker in the new refrigerator seems to be broken," he sounds like he is accusing me of treason. John's eyes are dark, and he is frowning. He looks at our guests.

"Okay, well that would be a problem," I reply nonchalantly, trying not to read too much into his tone. I had worked hard this week to make sure everything was taken care of for this party. I could not have predicted the new refrigerator's ice maker breaking. I look down and notice that he has his keys in his hand.

"Are you gonna run up to the gas station?" I ask. I feel like I should say something, maybe apologize for ice maker.

"Yes," John replies while leaning over to give me a quick peck on the cheek, the basket I am holding in front of me a barrier between us.

The kiss is fast, and he barely touches me. John never shows affection in public anymore. His action caught me off guard, and I am not prepared for this kiss. I want more. I want to fix this.

"I could go, or I could go with you, we could…" I try to say more, but John cuts me off. "I thought I would let Paul drive, since he has his learners," my husband says with a big smile on his face. He is not looking at me. He is watching Bill dance around the pool with one of the wives, Gloria. She is a pretty little thing in a short, strappy, red mini dress over her red white and blue bikini.

I notice John's entire demeanor changes as he watches them. I can tell he is thinking about something else. I try to focus on his words.

He wants to spend time with Paul. How could I refuse father-son bonding time when they had so little of that this year? Even if we had a yard full of his guests, they would only be gone for a quick trip, a few minutes down the road and back. It is important for them to spend time together; in a few years, Paul will be off to college.

I nod my head yes and respond, "Good idea. Maybe tonight you and I could talk about a few things. What we have going on? What our plans are for the summer? I was thinking, maybe we could take a vacation…go the beach." I smile up at my husband. He is still not looking at me. He is sending a text on his phone. He did not hear me.

My heart lurches. I am trying so hard to get John's attention. I sigh.

I know taking Paul is a terrific idea. After he finishes the message, I try to reach for John's hand, but he moves it away and puts his phone in his pocket quickly.

John steps back from me. He looks like he is remembering where he is. His smile is gone. I want to ask about the text message. Everyone he knows is here.

"John, who are you texting?" I start to ask. He jumps in, talking over me.

"Stella," he says quietly looking at me, "thanks for all this. It has been really good day. I am sure this is exactly what my career needs—a shot in the arm of camaraderie—to help me get some recognition. The troops will be talking up this party for weeks. You are a terrific military wife."

I lean closer into John, smelling his cologne. I do not recognize it. He smells good. My next thought is to try and steal a kiss. I feel like I should just let my non responded to text message go and move on. We are not teenagers and I do not need the added drama.

"Paul!" John barks out before I can move in. "Come drive your old man over to the store really quick." John moves around closer to where Paul is as he shouts, side stepping me and the basket I am holding. The moment for a kiss has evaporated. I am going to have to try harder to get John's attention if I want it.

Paul, dressed in navy blue swim trunks and an academy white baseball T-shirt looks up from the ping pong table where he is watching the action, smiles at us, and bounds over. His long legs make easy strides across the grass and onto the deck. He is such a good kid. His hair is getting a little long in the back, I notice, like a mom. I make a mental note to schedule a haircut for when school lets out next week. Moving the basket to my hip, I give Paul a little hug as he approaches us. He smells of pool chlorine and sunscreen. I ruffle his brown hair as he steps passed me, reaching for the keys in his dad's hands. They click together like a small bell or a chime that is slightly broken or off key. I look at them both. It makes me happy seeing them standing there together.

"Hold on," I say. "Before you go, I want a picture." I grab my iPhone from the back pocket of my black shorts and snap one quick shot before they get away. "Okay you two, hurry back. Be safe. I love you," I blurt out, embarrassing them both in front of our guests.

"Ahh, Mom! We are just running up to the store," Paul whines in response to my comment.

"I know," I reply, "but I can never say it enough." I laugh at him. "Someday, when you have kids, you will understand."

"Geez, I love you too, Mom," Paul blurts out as he disappears into the house to grab his wallet.

John stands there for a minute, silently looking across his backyard. He is back to watching the couples dancing and laughing by the pool. Bill has lifted his partner up and is joking about tossing her in the pool if he does not get a kiss on the cheek.

I look up at John. He is smiling again.

I will never get used to how good looking he is.

I start my mantra in my head. Counting my blessings.

I have the perfect little family.

I remind myself how lucky I am, how much I love our life here in Fayetteville in our beautiful home.

I keep repeating it.

"See you in a few. I'll hold down the fort here," I say to John as he turns and walks inside. He does not reply. He does not look at me.

It will all be okay, I tell myself.

I try not to read into the fact that he did not answer me. John only needs a beat to adjust to being home this time. We have been though rough patches before. Sixteen years of marriage did not come without a few bumps.

I look at my phone. I change my screen saver to the picture I took of John and Paul a few minutes ago. I notice that John never answered my text from this morning—the one I sent him from our bed. I try to think of something else, anything other than whomever he was texting before he left.

I am starting to recognize that the text, specifically whomever is on the other end, may be a problem. John is very distracted. I don't want to jump to conclusions, but my heart cannot help it.

I know deployments are hard on the guys. Everything I read says to give them some time to adjust to returning stateside. Our life at home is much different than what they live like when they are in the Middle East.

I turn back to our guests and decide to grab a Mike's Hard Lemonade from the blue cooler on the side of the deck, slamming the top back down with my new silver sandals. The hard thump sound makes me feel better.

I head down to sit by the pool and converse with the adults. A happy patriotic song is booming through the backyard. I grab on to the song to pull me back to the party. I start to sing along; the music inspires me. I am pushing the happy feelings up to cover my disappointment in John, in the lack of attention that I am getting from my husband. Texting and smiling at your phone and then hiding it in your pocket is never a good sign when your wife is standing right next to you watching. I am not stupid.

I am angry.

I am cute and sexy, damnit! I deserve a kiss and more.

I threw this whole damn party for him.

I am talking to John in my head better than I can manage in person lately. My singing turns into a hum as I weave my way through the guests. I am looking for a seat in the shade next to my husband's colonel, Steve, and his very new wife, Jane, from Texas.

Steve and Jane arrived late after everyone else. John had not looked happy to see them. I am confused by this as I thought the reason for the party was to impress his team and his bosses. John greeted them with a quick *hello* in the front hall before returning to the gang by the grill where he was telling stories. John left me to bring them to the backyard and get them situated as Jane tried to apologize about some to-do on post at the general's home that they had to attend first. The colonel went on to explain that they had already eaten as well. I noticed right away that they came overdressed for our pool party. Steve was wearing tan slacks and a soft yellow Hawaiian-type shirt, his big gold Rolex watch catching my eye. Jane was in a red, polka-dot sun dress with matching red high-heeled sandals. She smelled overly sweet, like lilacs and springtime. Her make-up and hair were perfectly done like they were here for a photo shoot instead of a pool party. Her new engagement ring and wedding band sparkled at me. I had heard the set was from the big jewelry store downtown in Fayetteville; the rings look amazing. That rock must have set Steve back a pretty penny; it was like something a movie star would wear. Jane and Steve stand out amongst the crowd in our backyard and are easy for me to spot.

I start toward the couple. They look hot and uncomfortable, drinking bottled water while all the other adults at the party are enjoying ice cold beers and the pitchers of margaritas. I feel like they are the King and the Queen passing judgement on the rest of us. I am waiting for the royal decree that it is okay to have fun or for one of them to crack a smile. The two of them are sitting on our white folding chairs under a tree away from the pool like they are on a time-out from the fun. Jane is scanning the crowd as if she is looking for something or someone. Steve looks like he cannot wait to leave. I notice they are not talking to each other. Maybe there is trouble in paradise there, too.

"I am glad you two could make it." I try to sound happy and smile at them as I pull up an empty folding chair next to Jane.

"You have put together a fantastic party, Stella." Jane smiles at me.

"Well, I thought we should stick our heads in the door since you and John were going to all this trouble for the unit," Steve replies politely while waving his hand around to indicate the crowd.

"No problem at all. It is important to John to bring everyone together today. Memorial Day is about the soldiers," I reply, trying to make eye contact.

Jane smiles and nods in agreement. The music fills the gap in our conversation.

"Can I get you two anything? We have some cake left," I offer. Jane reaches for Steve's hand.

"Honey, would you like to split a piece of cake with me?" Steve places his hand on top of hers.

"Not right now. I am full of lunch…That was a terrific Waldorf salad you brought to the General's home. I ate three servings."

They look at each other. I see that Jane appreciates his compliment. It is almost like I am watching an intimate moment the way Steve is caressing her hand.

I shift uncomfortably in my seat. Condensation drips from the glass bottle in my hand. I watch the drops disappear into the grass.

What next? Do I ask them about the weather?

My mind wanders to my problems with John. I want to take out my phone and try texting him, but that would be rude in front of this couple. Besides, I am not sure what I would say at this point. *I know you are texting somebody and they make you smile.* That is a dumb thing to text your husband or anyone. I need better facts or conclusions, and I think I need to wait to talk to him in person like a grown-up.

I try to distract myself by watching the kids play in the pool.

The overdressed couple next to me continues to hold hands, quietly watching the party, sipping their bottled water. The minutes tick slowly by. I drink my Mike's Hard Lemonade fast, the sour alcohol helping me relax as I search for a conversation topic or a reason to escape the happy couple.

Abruptly, a piercing, thunderous roar rips through the air, disturbing the house party. The world seems to tilt, and all other noise stops as the substantial eruption rocks the neighborhood. Everyone freezes and moves at once, as if someone hit the fast-forward button. Car alarms activate throughout the neighborhood, causing a cacophony of noise following the explosion. In that moment, all the happy sounds of the party are drowned out by vulgar, harsh noises that make no sense and baffle us. Living so close to Ft. Bragg, we are all used to a little rumble and shaking, but this is different. This is close, very close. Something is wrong. We all stand up and look to the sky, trying to find the source of the noise. I think I have bigger problems than who John is texting.

Chapter 5

We run to the front yard to find the source, and I am stopped in my tracks by the reality of what I come upon. Our Jeep is on fire at the end of our driveway. What I perceive to be a warzone is happening in my front yard. Fire, smoke and burnt metal are creating a scene that seems out of place in our pleasant neighborhood. I cannot understand what has happened, why there is fire, and what caused this chaos. I am immobile.

Within minutes, two fire trucks stop in front of my house with a great rush of sound. Three firemen jump down and pull hoses from the truck, attaching them to the fire hydrant in the neighbor's yard. Another fireman appears at the side of the truck, rushing toward John's Jeep with an axe and a fire extinguisher. Jane and I watch from the grass as my tears continue to fall. Our party-goers are now huddled to the side, grouped by family, watching the scene unfold. I can see the neighbors across the street holding their children's hands as they exclaim about the firetrucks on our street. It is a big day for our quiet neighborhood.

Firefighters work to extinguishing the fire quickly. I watch a mist of smoke that continues to circle upwards. It is as if I am viewing this as a spectator to a live movie event, not something that is happening to me. Jane carefully pulls me back off the grass to our front porch, off to the side and away from our guests, as the firemen spray down the area surrounding the Jeep.

Someone thinks to turn off the firetruck's sirens. The absence of the noise is deafening. I feel like I am in a dream.

City Police cars arrive on the street as the fire is put out. Police begin creating a perimeter around the front of the house, blocking us in. There is an ambulance on the street as well, and a crew in paramedic uniforms stands to the side, waiting to help. For all the fire and destruction, there are no bodies, and no one is hurt. A police officer walks up to a few of our pool party attendees, the military guys closest to the jeep, addressing the crowd.

"Whose house is this?" he asks. "Can someone tell me what happened?"

A few of John's soldiers step forward, pushing their families behind them. They identify themselves and point to me; I hear the words party, explosion, fire, and no bodies float across the front lawn. The police officer is taking notes while a second officer hangs yellow crime scene tape around the Jeep. Another man dressed in civilian clothes and carrying a badge brings the tape up to the front porch, tying it off by using the front pillars.

They are everywhere, scurrying like ants, doing their job and securing the scene. An older gentleman, dressed in civilian clothes, seems to be in charge. He walks through the yard, speaking to a few of the officers. He stops next to the police officer taking notes, asks him a few questions, and walks towards me. He enters the front porch without looking back at the Jeep.

"Ma'am, I am Detective Horace Johnson. I understand you are the owner of the home. And that was your husband's Jeep? Would you mind stepping inside and answering a few questions for me?" His southern drawl reminds me of Morgan Freeman in *Driving Miss Daisy*. It is comforting and confident. Jane stands next to me. I can feel her readiness to jump in and help.

"I am Stella Finch, and this is my home," my voice is shakier than I intend.

I step forward, unsure of my legs, as Jane pulls open the screen door. Detective Johnson enters the house first. His tan slacks and blue button-down shirt seem like a uniform and easy set of work clothes for a man called out at a moment's notice.

"Ma'am, is your husband at home? Is anyone in the house?" he asks looking around.

We walk into the front sitting room, and I sit on the edge of one of our wingback chairs. I stare at his big, brown Rockport shoes, nothing John would ever wear. He would call them old man shoes. Normally, I would offer him a seat or ask to get him a glass of water or iced tea.

Jane stands to the side of my chair. I can still feel her presence.

"Detective Johnson, I do not know where my husband is. He left our pool party to run up the street with my son, Paul, to get ice…Paul was driving; was going to drive. He recently got his learner's permit. John…John was worried that we were out of ice. The new ice maker in the refrigerator stopped working, and we had all of these guests over. It was hot. John and Paul left. I don't know where they are…" my voice trails off.

I look at the detective for answers.

"Mrs. Finch would you excuse me for a minute? I'll be right back with you," he quickly walks from the room.

"Of course," I respond as if he is a friend that stopped by for a chat. I sit there looking at my wedding rings as he walks out of the front door. I see the detective call the other officers to the center of my front yard. I watch them talk through the front window. The crime tape is now fluttering in the breeze like a ribbon. It reminds me of the yellow ribbons that were tied around the trees of military families and people in their communities when soldiers were deployed years ago for *Desert Storm*. I had always thought it was a nice gesture, but now I feel the yellow ribbons mean something darker.

Detective Johnson comes back in the front door. He moves faster than before.

"Mrs. Finch, to clarify, your husband and son are missing? Your husband, Major John Evan Finch in the Army Special Forces Unit stationed at Ft. Bragg, and your son, Paul Jonathan Finch, left approximately fifteen minutes ago to drive down the street for ice? Since that time, approximately 3:10 pm, you have not seen or heard from either of them?" The detective's questions sound like he is repeating a drill. The questions are coming at me fast.

"No, I have not seen John or Paul since they left for ice," I reply.

"Okay, ma'am, we have sent a car down the street to the gas station to check if they got there with someone else's vehicle. Would they have gone somewhere else?" he asks.

I sit there and think about that for a minute. Where would they have gone? I look at Detective Johnson's hands holding his notebook. He is wearing a wedding ring, a plain gold band. My brain is having a tough time thinking of where else John and Paul would go for ice.

"No, they would have gone there for ice," I reply. I start to twist my wedding band. A knock sounds on the screen door and I jump.

A short, stocky soldier in a Military Police uniform, an MP, walks into the room; he looks and walks like a body builder.

"Hello, Mrs. Finch. I am Detective Soto from Ft. Bragg. I was called to your home to help." Detective Soto and Detective Johnson greet each other. Detective Johnson motions for Soto to follow him outside.

Again, I hear, "Mrs. Finch please excuse us for a minute."

I look back out the window from my perch on the chair and watch the men talking. Another group of men joins them. Across the yard, I can see other officers talking to the pool party guests. There could be a hundred people standing on my front lawn. Red fire trucks, black and white police cars, and other unfamiliar cars are all blocking the street. It looks like a parade or circus.

I think about the backyard. I wonder about the cake we left out and all the food. I stare at my rings. I lean back in the navy-blue wing chair, letting it swallow me up. I am trying not to worry about John and Paul because, if I do, I will go crazy. I cannot answer the questions going through my head. I sit forward, and I stare at the Jeep; black and burnt at the end of the driveway. My mind does not have the answers. I forgot Jane was standing by my side until she speaks up, "Stella, can I get you some water, maybe something else to drink?" she asks.

"Sure," I respond. I don't really care at this point. "The kitchen is right through there," I point.

Jane walks off, leaving me alone. A woman with short, black hair walks in the house. She is wearing black slacks and a white button-down shirt. She looks around and stops when she sees me.

"Mrs. Finch, I am FBI Officer Jennifer Scott from the Fayetteville field office attached to Ft. Bragg. I want to ask you a few questions." She shows me her credentials. I see the men still talking in the yard.

"Mrs. Finch, where is your husband, Major John Evan Finch?" she asks.

I stare at her, noticing the small pearl earrings in her ears. She has no other jewelry on. I have no answer to her question.

"I do not know, Agent Scott," I respond. I am getting angry. All of these people and no one is doing anything. All they want to do is question me. I make a fist at my side.

"Mrs. Finch, was something wrong with your Jeep? Why did it catch fire in your yard?" the Agent asks while looking at her phone.

"I don't think anything was wrong with the Jeep. How would I know?" I reply. I want to shout. I cover my face with my hands. Jane walks back into the room holding my water. She greets Agent Scott. I look up, take my water from Jane, and set it carefully on the side table next to me without drinking it.

Jane breaks the silence by saying, "A few of the wives are cleaning up the backyard. They are going to put the leftover food in your refrigerator and cover the cake. Is there anything else you need them to do?" she asks. I sit there and stare at her.

"No," I respond.

I don't know what the proper response is when you have explosion in your front yard and your family goes missing. Should I ask them to stay? Offer everyone a beer? Laughter bubbles up inside me at the absurdity. I do not know the proper protocol for explosions. I wanted today to be prefect; this is the opposite.

Detectives Johnson and MP Soto walk back in. They seem surprised to see Agent Scott. Detective Johnson looks at me.

"Mrs. Finch, we are going to let your guests leave and take their children home. We have questioned everyone and collected their information." One of fire trucks and the ambulance start to pull away from the house.

"I see," Agent Scott says. "Gentleman, can I talk to you outside, please?" It sounded more like a command than a question.

All three go back out the door, leaving me with Jane. I watch out the front window as families start to get in their cars to leave. Our pool party is over. *John got his wish—people will be talking about this for a long time.* One little boy is holding one of our bright-colored beach balls as he follows his family down the street to their vehicle. I think about Paul at that age. I sit there for what seems like hours thinking about Paul as a baby, Paul starting school, Paul playing ball; my Paul growing up. The worry is building up inside me. I try to push it down. I walk to the door and step out, joining the team of investigators. They are arguing.

"*Does anyone know where my family is?*" I shout at them. The detectives, officers and agents in my front yard all stop and turn to look at me. No one answers.

"*I need to know where John and Paul are,*" I shout, slowly pronouncing every syllable.

No one steps up and helps me. Everyone is trying to figure out what happened, what to do next, who is in charge. No one seems to care about me and my questions. I am a part of their investigation, a means to an end, a way to get their questions answered; but I have no answers. I need answers. John and Paul have been missing for three hours. I check my phone for updates and realize it is dead. I want to throw it.

Three hours. John and Paul. Three Hours.

I run over to the family with the little boy and stop the dad. I remember his name is Joe. "Joe, is there anything the unit can do to help me find John and

Paul. Where is Colonel Steve? Could you find him for me, maybe put a search team together?" I am near breaking.

I do not know what to do. Joe looks at me. "Ma'am, I am sure the authorities have this under control. They look really organized. I have not seen Colonel Steve since the explosion. Maybe ask his wife, Jane? She was in your kitchen last I saw. I need to get my family home. My little boy and wife, they have been really troubled by all this, and I need to take care of them." He raises his arms and pats me on the back.

I understand. I nod my head at him. "Go, Joe, take care of your family. I understand."

I wave at them already seated in the car with their seat belts on they look scared and tired. Joe turns and gets into his car. I stand silently, watching him drive away with his family. I am lost.

Jane is watching me from the front porch.

As I approach, Jane offers to stay and sit with me. I decline with a shake of my head. Her husband, the Colonel, comes up to stand next to her.

"Steve, is there anything the unit can do? Can I come with you to Ft. Bragg and go through John's desk? Maybe there is a file or something there that can help," I plead.

"No, Stella, I already have someone at the unit looking at John's work. It is all classified files. You would not be allowed," Steve's voice is cold.

Jane moves in and hugs me.

"If you need anything, call me. You have my cell phone number."

I am grateful for her friendship. She hands me a bottle of water from the pool party. I turn the bottle slowly in my hand, my wedding band appearing through the bottle as if it is a foreign object. It is distorted and unclear. Nothing feels right. Steve stands there looking at me. I think he is going to say something reassuring; instead, he takes Jane's hand and moves past me.

Steve and Jane leave. I watch their car pull away from the house from the front porch. All of the party-goers have now gone. I go in, closing the front door behind me. I am trying to piece together everything that has happened today, but all I can do is worry about Paul.

Chapter 6

I feel hollow. I know I am in shock. I need answers, and I want my family back in one piece. I think back to before John and Paul left for the ice run. Are there any clues I am missing?

I play with my wedding ring and try to figure out how to breathe in and out.

The teams of investigators continue to ask me questions. It is like we are playing a guessing game with no rules and no winner.

What has been recovered from the fire in the driveway is essentially nothing. No bodies. The investigators, the police, the FBI, they have no leads. An accelerant was poured on the Jeep to start the fire. It seems John and Paul were taken before that happened. Less than 6 hours ago, people were happy, but we were out of ice. Who cares about ice?

Oh my God, John and Paul.

My brain freezes trying not to think of the worst scenarios. I have to have hope. I have to find them. I keep thinking about the day. It started with drama that I made up in my head about my marriage and my needs and wanting to have sex...

Now...John and Paul are gone. *Where could they be? Is this a military army thing or a weird neighbor or some random act of crazy serial killer?* My mind spins.

It all happened too rapidly, but the pain and confusion seem to go on. Afterwards, after the explosion and the fire are out, the fire chief tries to explain to me what that was in my front yard; the chaos, the flames, "the event" as they are calling it.

The police investigator, the Military police, the FBI—they all talk at me about the event in my front yard. None of it makes sense. Why would John and Paul go with someone away from me, away from our pool party with all our guests, without telling me what was going on, without contacting me to let me know they are okay? Agent Scott of the FBI stated that something could have been wrong with the Jeep, like a massive recall on exploding engines, but that idea makes no sense. A picture of Jeeps exploding in driveways across America enters my mind. It's a cartoon image like on the Simpsons. It would make a bizarre evening news story—*Self-Combusting Jeeps; our lead story at 6.*

There will be an investigation, I keep being told. The military is sending more people out; the city police had sent people out; the FBI in Washington would be in contact. I have been told not to talk to anyone. People in uniforms were walking around my home, around my yard, crawling around in the remains of John's Jeep. I want to scream at them all that they are wrong, and they need to leave. No one needs to investigate us. They need to go and find my family.

I fixate on John and his military career. I sit there, staring at my wedding ring, in the front room where they left me. My heart is breaking for Paul. The safety of our son is tearing me apart.

I want to go back to the time before the party. Before any of this. I am shattered. I try to remember to breathe in and out. I run a hand through my hair. *I can do this. I can push forward and help find the answers. I can help find my family, no matter what it takes.* I stand in the front room, wiping tears from my eyes.

Suddenly there is a knock at the door. Jake and some of Paul's baseball teammates come through the door with their parents. One of the boys is holding a casserole. It is what we do in the South, bring food when people are sick or sad. Everybody says they want to help, but they truly want to know if I heard anything. Lots of hugs are exchanged. It could have been a party except for the tears and the sad faces. Nothing matters to me except understanding what happened. I am supposed to feel grateful that these people are here and glad that so many showed up this evening. I accept the casserole, and I am glad when everyone starts to leave. I hug Jake, thanking him for coming. It makes me feel closer to Paul.

John and I do not have any extended family left both of our parents have passed away in the last few years. The army has been our family, our connection for holidays and family events. As an only child, of two only children Paul has created his own extended family with his baseball team and school friends. Jake is like a brother to Paul.

The word *gone* continues to bounce around in my head. We do not belong to a church, but I feel the need to pray. I always meant to go to church. Somehow, we always got off track. Family time, things to do or errands to run. John is deployed a lot, and when he is home, he is not very interested in church. My mind is wandering, thinking about all the deployments, John's time away, and all the wasted time. All this thinking and waiting, I want to scream and run out the door, search the neighborhood and yell their names like I am looking for a lost dog.

I want to shout, "Bags of ice! My life has changed because of some *goddamn ice*!"

I want my family back. I hold on to the gold heart that Paul had given me for Mother's Day many years ago. It sits on the chain around my neck, and the metal feels cool and slick beneath my fingers. I grip it tightly, as if I can reach Paul through it. I try to remember to breathe in and out. I try to figure out what I need to do next, where I need to go to find Paul and John.

I look down at the floor to the silver sandals on my feet. I had bought them with Paul on our trip up to South Point mall last week when we ate too much cheesecake. I want my son back. The pain that hits my heart as I think of him makes me double over. It is too much to bear.

I look around the room. It is empty; I am alone. I push the fingernail from my index finger into the base of my thumb to feel pain. It is like I am checking to see if I am still here. I feel it, but it does not compare with the ache in my chest. I think about who would want to destroy my perfect family. It makes no sense to me. We are good people. MP Soto has mentioned that the army will be sending over a counselor to speak with me, but because of the holiday weekend they are having trouble getting someone here quickly. I am not really concerned about that; *what would I say to them anyway*, I upset and anxious like any normal mother. I am out of my mind with worry.

Paul! I cry out to the room. I hit the door with my fist. The thump echoes in my heart.

Out the front window, there is a police officer stationed on the porch. I can see that the neighborhood is mostly empty, and a rosy glow is filling the sky. The day will be over soon. Birds perch in the trees like little families gathering for the night. I scan the rest of the road out my front window. All the cars are gone except one—a very serious-looking, tall, Indian man is standing across the street in front of a neighbor's house. He gazes at me while leaning on the

41

driver's door of an older model, beige, four-door Honda. I gaze back at him. Do I know him? Is he in John's unit? I shake my head. No, I do not think so.

A cloud passes over the setting sun, leaving me standing in a dark shadow. I have no answers for the investigators. They are still in the backyard looking for clues or standing in my dining room, talking to their superiors on their smartphones. This is a big case; they keep telling me. A priority with all their departments. I am not feeling comforted by their words. I am sinking in pain like it is mud around me capturing me, swallowing me, sticking to me until it is all I can see and feel.

I look out to where the dark-skinned man with the beige Honda had been. He is no longer there. The neighborhood is completely empty now. The birds have stopped chirping. Our life and the beautiful new home that we built in Fayetteville is in turmoil. John and Paul are missing, and I am still here with no answers. I do not know what to do. Nothing feels right.

I go to check my phone and social media to see if I have any word from John or Paul. I forgot that the investigators have it in the dining room. They have taken it from me for the investigation and to tie it into their systems in case of a phone call from the kidnappers. My stomach is in knots. I dry heave against the chair. It is 9 pm according to the clock on the wall. John and Paul have been missing for almost 6 hours.

I move to watch the investigators in my dining room typing on their laptops. I am invisible to them. They are working an important case. There are answers here somewhere. I wish I knew more about John's work and what he was doing for the last six months.

Chapter 7

In the kitchen, I stuff a few double stuff Oreo cookies into my stomach and gulp a big glass of red wine as I wander about the kitchen looking at all the upgrades and little details, I had spent too much time picking out. These are the things I thought were important over the last year. I am frustrated with myself. I am angry with John for being gone so much. I should have been spending more time with Paul. I berate myself. I pull open the kitchen junk drawers looking for clues about John. I move through the house opening closets like a stranger investigating my own home. Somewhere there must be something that will help, that will explain what happened here today.

A news crew shows up around 10 pm. They are a little late to the party. Detective Johnson and MP Soto go out to speak with them on the front lawn, telling them this is a matter of national security, and send them away for now.

The investigators ask me the same questions repeatedly. I am pretty sure I am going to throw-up the Oreos and red wine. My head is spinning. They suck up all of my energy. I am waiting for something to happen, like when a kidnapping happens in the movies and a special team sets up a command center and taps your phone. Then the kidnappers call telling you their demands for millions of dollars and the FBI special team tracks the call. None of that is happening here. The investigators try to explain to me that, because of John's military background, they are not treating this like a normal kidnapping. We would not be making any appeals on television for their safe return. Besides, I was told they could tap our phones without setting up a command center like on TV. In fact, they did not even need to be here to do that.

The FBI investigators explain that they have to handle this through special government channels. They feel this is about national security, and they hope I understand. If this gets my family back, they can send smoke signals to aliens if that is what they need to do. I am trusting them to do their best. I feel like my life depends on it. I move on to searching my bedroom and bathroom.

Opening John's aftershave, I notice his new bottle of cologne on the counter. I pick it up, sliding my hands over the bottle. I open it and smell it. I can picture John this morning standing on the deck, working on his grills.

I look for any sign of John and Paul. Mostly, I try to remember to breathe. I have to stop myself from looking out the front door at the explosion site. Like somehow, by my force of will, I can make John and Paul appear if I stand there. Bits and pieces fly back to me anyway, hitting me like flashes, showing me what had been taken from me. Each time my stomach reacts violently. My emotions are thrashing through me, stormy and dark.

I try to stay positive, to look for signs that this is all a big mistake, a nightmare that I can awaken from and it will all disappear. I cannot take it anymore. I walk out of my house and stand on the charred ground looking back at my home. I stand on the ground where Paul and John were before they were gone. I check the ground for pieces of them even though I know they are not here. It is dark as I grope for answers. The street lights my only guide. The police detective stationed on the front porch comes over to talk to me, he understands, but I need to go back in the house. Reluctantly, I go inside leaving the last place my family was known to be safe.

I decide to close all the blinds and curtains in the house. I move from room to room quickly. I do not want to have contact with the outside, my neighbors whose lives are continuing, whose husband and child did not leave them for an ice run. I do not want to experience the dogwood trees, flowers, or green grass in the backyard. I feel like the green grass is mocking me, reminding me of events from earlier in the day.

As it gets closer to midnight, the investigators are all getting fatigued. The excitement of the day is wearing off. Nothing is happening that I can tell. No big announcements are happening, only quiet, shifty conversations across the room. I cannot watch them ignore me. I know they are running out of official talking points. Their big case is not as exciting as it was to them earlier in the day.

It has been 9 hours since the explosion. I feel like the clock is ticking loudly, and I am the only one who hears it.

I move to my bedroom. I stand there and think of this morning, of Paul running in trying to find his sandals. Of his asking me about the road trip with Jake. I would let him go anywhere with his friend if I could get him back. The image makes me smile and tears start to fall again.

I rip the comforter off the bed. The decorative pillows fall to the floor. I do not move to pick them up. I wrap the blanket around me as I head into John's closet, hiding away from the images running through my mind. I curl in a ball on the floor of his closet, using the comforter from our bed. The space feels safe from the unknown monsters that stole my family away from me this afternoon; their faceless shapes taking over my mind. The closet and the comforter do not help. I cry big, wet tears painful tears that rack my body and heart in my chest. I cry until I cannot. I close my eyes and try to rest. The images behind my eyelids are too painful.

I look up and fixate on John's army uniforms hanging stiffly. They are lined up and perfectly pressed. I start to tug on them. Ripping them from the hangers. I know John's disappearance has something to do with his job. Tops and bottoms start to gather around me. I am angry at the army for taking him away from me all these years. For taking John away from Paul. The hangers rock empty of all the pieces. Some are tangled, others have fallen to join me in the mess. I look at the name and rank tags and the buttons, running my hands around these pieces that John wore every day. I want to tear them apart. In the breast pocket of one of his shirts, under his name, I feel a small piece of paper. It is folded over. Maybe it is a lost laundry tag or a sewing receipt. I reach in and carefully pull out the small white rectangle.

I unfold it. The paper is from a hotel. On the top is the logo of hotel. The name is swirled around palm trees *Amanjena Resort*. The lettering is pretty. I let my finger touch the name of the hotel. Underneath the logo is an address in Marrakech, Morocco. I had always wanted to go there. I stare at the paper. It has been refolded several times. My eyes travel to the words written in black ink on the center.

Thanks for the picnic

 Rain

More tears start to fall. They hit the folded paper. I know what the problem is in my marriage now. I crumble the paper and shove it back into the pocket. It won't go in, so I force it, pushing and pulling the pocket with a growl of frustration. The anger comes. I kick John's clothes away from me. I am frantic to get his things off of me. Finally, I am alone on the comforter.

I sit there and stare at the wall.

I am crushed. The weight of the hurt slams into my heart.

The love, the want, the need, all of me that I have been nurturing like an olive branch reaching for John withers away. I thought about all I had come to take for granted like I knew he traveled to the Middle East on a regular basis. I had gotten used to the fact that his job was dangerous and there were things he could not share, but this betrayal smashed me into pieces.

Too tired to sleep, too sad to move. I realize the party never mattered. No matter how great the party was, John would not have been mine. The piece of paper does not lie. The paper added to his text messages and his lack of interest in me show me what I did not want to know.

John is having an affair...with a woman named Rain.

Around 3 am, I drag the blanket, grabbing a few pillows, and prepare a nest on the couch in the den. I grab my phone from the kitchen where I had plugged it in and switch on the television; the investigators had handed me back the phone hours ago. I flip from the local news to the national news to reruns of cooking shows and back again. I start to Google Amanjena Resort and Marrakech, Morocco.

I cannot sleep in our bedroom tonight.

My mind focuses on John's note with the heart from Rain that he kept in the breast pocket of his jacket. Near his heart. I start to stalk Facebook and Google for women named Rain in Morocco.

I need answers.

I continue to flip channels on the TV. I can hear the investigators in the dining room moving around. I am not ready to share John's note with them.

Eventually, I doze-off for an hour during an episode on the Food Network on grilling vegetables. For a second, when I open my eyes, I think that everything is good, that life has returned to before we ran out of ice. Lost in confusion, I find myself in the den wearing yesterday's pool party clothes, holding my phone.

Reality hits me hard, like someone has slammed into the back of my car at a red light. It hurts all over. I am angry and devastated all at the same time.

Looking in the dining room, I can see the investigation team left sometime during the night only to return in fresh clothes. I don't know how long I sit in the den listening to them work in the dining room. I listen to them send out reports on laptops, answer their phones, and track down information that all turns into zero leads. Eventually, I move from the couch to the kitchen, where I throw things away that had been stored in the refrigerator from the party, tossing each item one-by-one in the trash with a thud. I look at the Walmart cake on the island, pick it up and take it into the investigators sitting in the dining room. I lay it on the buffet table off to the side. I try to think of something to ask, but I can tell no one has news. They all look away when I enter. I want to stomp my feet and get their attention.

I return to the kitchen pantry and bring them a stack of paper plates, napkins, and forks. I am not being nice. I am getting rid of the cake. I don't say anything, and they don't offer any information. Back in the kitchen, I stand there, and I realize that someone had wiped down all the counters and put everything away from yesterday. Even my wine glass from last night has been put away. It looks like nothing has happened here. Instead of feeling happy that someone cleaned up, I am angry, I want everyone to leave my world alone. It is my family and my home.

It's 8 am, and I start to make a pot of coffee. I lay a few coffee cups on the counter, taking out the creamer and Stevia like I am taking care of guests. I am doing these things without thinking; it is automatic. Life is moving forward, no matter what I do. I pick up my blue coffee mug and hold it—it was my favorite only yesterday—and I throw it against the wall. It is the one of a set I bought at the mall with Paul only last week, fun times that are no more.

It shatters with a loud crash, the pieces falling to the floor.

An agent I had not met sticks his head in the kitchen, sees the broken mug, and goes to pick it up off the floor, starting to ask if I am okay. I raise my hand to stop him. I do not have the words.

I feel like a criminal trespassing in our happy home, alone with these strangers working in the other room. Jane, Colonel Steve's wife, calls to check on me. I don't want to tell her, but John's affair comes pouring out. I tell her about the note, his text messages, our lack of sex life. I talk and she listens. I want to ask her to speak to Steve. To ask him about the note in John's pocket. But something stops me from asking for Steve's help. Maybe it was his cold attitude yesterday, but I feel like I need to protect myself from him.

Jane is kind and listens. She tells me the note is probably nothing—a work thing—and not to worry. John loves me. I hang-up, thanking her for her help, but I am not ready to let the fact that John had an affair die.

I stop back in the den and continue to listen to the investigation and wait for answers. I have the TV still on in the background as a distraction. A neighbor drops off another casserole. Detective Johnson answers the door and takes the casserole from them on the front porch. He brings it in to me.

"Ma'am, do you want me to put this in the kitchen with the other one?" he asks.

"No, take it into the team," I reply, not caring what happens to it. "Detective, has the team dumped my husband's cell phone? I mean, do they have his text messages and phone calls? Do they know where he has been recently and who he has been talking to?"

Detective Johnson looks at me and takes in a slow breath.

"Yes, ma'am. We have the information from his phone, and we know where he has been. The military and FBI are tracing back all leads. We have also gotten all the information from your son's phone, too."

They know who John has been texting. Where John has been. I am embarrassed as he waits for my next question. I am not going to ask who my husband has been texting. I do not want to hear about Rain.

Everyone knows. I turn away embarrassed. I decide to go into our office. John has not used the room in forever, but we keep an old laptop plugged in on the desk. Mostly, I file the bills here and keep track of the house remodeling stuff. I open John's laptop. His screen saver is a picture of Washington D.C. It looks like a cell phone photo of the White House taken in the rain from a few blocks away. The picture is an odd choice to me. I am not sure what it means. I notice there is nothing in the search history that jumps out at me. No clues to John's life away from home. John never really used social media, he does not have a Facebook or Twitter account. He had said it was not a good fit for his work when I asked him if he wanted me to set him up on Facebook so we could tag him in family photos. I start to go through the files and papers on the desk. Most of them are mine, house related. I am looking for anything that helps me find Paul. In a few hours, I am surrounded by papers. I realize how much money I have spent on remodeling and decorating. The dollars really add up. I am no closer to finding John and Paul. I take the laptop to Detective Johnson, maybe there is something there I am missing. Something there that will help them locate my family.

At 3 pm on Tuesday, almost exactly 24 hours since John and Paul had gone missing and the event had happened in my front yard, the investigation team of the Fayetteville Police, the Fort Bragg Military Police, and the FBI let me know they would be leaving to go back to work in their offices. They are going to leave a police presence outside watching the house, maybe stationed on the front porch or in a car out front. There has been no contact from the kidnappers, and they are not expecting anything new to turn-up here. Together, the three investigators I had met first yesterday, Johnson, Soto and Scott, fill up the small space in the den where I have been sitting. It feels like I have known them longer than 24 hours. Their faces and names are etched into my heart as the first people to talk to me and begin the search for John and Paul.

They have no leads, but they will continue to work the case. I stand there, staring at them. I have nothing to say. I do not want to thank them for being here, and I cannot thank them for leaving. They have done nothing; my family is still missing. I have no answers. I cannot believe they are leaving when the job is not done. I reflect on those television kidnap shows where they move in with the command center and find the missing person in a one-hour episode; I want one of that kind of team here at my house helping me find John and Paul. I feel angry and I want to lash out at them for being calm and professional when my life is crashing down around me into utter chaos.

Detective Johnson stops before me, taking my hand.

"Thank you for the cake and casserole. Please make sure to leave the yellow crime tape where it is since this is an active investigation. If you have any questions, please call me. I have left my card on your kitchen counter by the coffee machine. Is there someone you can stay with? Somewhere you can go so you are not alone?"

"No, we have no immediate family, John and I were only children. Our parents have passed; the army is our family. I would rather stay here in my home, with my things, where my family was…" I trail off.

He releases my hand. MP Soto speaks next. He tells me that he will be working with John's unit. Agent Scott gets a phone call while MP Soto is talking and heads back to the dining room where her laptop is located. Everyone packs up and leaves.

Agent Scott looks at me and continues to talk on her phone as she leaves. There are no goodbyes or hugs; this is not a dinner party. I do not stand at the front door and wave them off. I am mad about their lack of progress. I walk through the house and check all the doors, making sure they are locked behind them. At the end of the day, I am no good to Paul if something happens to me.

I inspect my empty dining room the team vacated. They had reset the space. I push in a chair that is sticking out a little bit making it even with the others. It all looks like the last 24 hours had not happened; like it was nightmare or a figment of an active imagination.

I run my hand across the corner of the dining room table where for the last day, a team of highly skilled investigators had been trying to find my family. I wish somehow the table could give me the answers that the team could not. I stand there trying to imagine what they learned, and the leads they did not share with me. The data they downloaded from our devices. The trail they might have picked up.

Nothing comes to me. I shake my head at myself.

My life is not a sci-fi movie, the table is not going to give me the answers, and it looks like neither are the investigators.

I glance down at my black shorts and white T-shirt. I am still wearing my pool party clothes.

I push myself to take a shower.

The hot water helps me. I feel a little more human.

After my shower, I pull on a pair of comfy pajama pants saved for Netflix binge watching and pizza nights, adding a "mom's love baseball" T-shirt. I turn on the TV in the bedroom to the local news and lay across the sheets.

The comforter is still in the den. The decorative pillows are scattered across the floor. Keeping my home neat and tidy is not on my to-do list anymore.

I see John's closet door open and all his clothes laying haphazardly on the floor. I turn away and stare at the ceiling, willing myself not to cry over John as I lay on our bed.

I feel another level of sadness and frustration wash over me. I want to hit him.

I want to yell and fight, to have it out.

Instead, I am wandering around like a ghost praying for his and my son's safe return. I grab a fistful of sheets in my hand and pull.

The contrast of the emotions rolling around inside me is tearing me apart.

I want a man to love me. I want to be loved. I am loveable damnit!

I feel selfish worrying about myself and my marriage with Paul missing. I pull the sheets around me, embracing myself.

I reach for my phone, scrolling through the apps, hoping for some word from the detectives, a lead to Paul's whereabouts.

Nothing.

I grab John's pillow and throw it across the room. It hits the wall and slumps to the floor. I take my pillow and tuck it under my head. Within minutes, I am asleep, alone in my home.

I sleep only for a few hours. I wake-up staring at John's closet. The clothes on the floor, the empty hangers.

I notice his luggage on the shelf above. I get up from the bed and move over to the closet, flipping on the light. I take down his bags and start to unzip them. The investigators had been through the house, but it does not look like they touched these. Opening them up and checking the pockets. In the top back zipper pocket, I find receipts for the last few months. They are all for cities in the Middle East, including Marrakech. I go over each receipt, look at the dates and places. I cannot read most of the writing, but my heart understands. I study the receipts for a long time. These small pieces of paper tell me a story of what John has been doing for the last six months. Going out to eat, buying wine, and taking trips.

When I am done torturing myself, I place the receipts on John's nightstand in a neat stack. I lay back down on the bed and think about my life, my marriage, and my son. I worry about Paul. I check my phone, scrolling through my social media for hints about what is going on. I fall asleep trying to figure out what John's affair has to do with his disappearance.

I wake-up to the sound of my phone ringing. It is lying next to me on the bed. I am tangled in the sheets. I hit the answer button. My heart is racing. This could be news. I sit up straight putting my feet on the floor. I am shaking. I can barely hold my phone.

"Stella, this is Agent Scott with the FBI. I have been looking into your husband's finances and recent travel. I have a few questions for you. Can you come into our office this morning? We are by the mall across from Carrabba's Italian Restaurant in the office building. I can text you the address. Does 10 am work for you?" the agent sounds very professional.

My mind is racing when I answer, "Yes, I can be there. Do I need to bring our checkbook or bank statement?" My head hurts. My mouth feels like it's full of cotton. I cannot remember the last time I drank any water.

"No," she responds very perfunctorily.

I look at the bedside clock. Numbers are there looking at me. It takes a moment for me to see them.

It is 8 am. I am waiting for Agent Scott to say something else, and I finally realize she is not going to speak again.

"Is there any news on the whereabouts of Paul and John?" I want the answer to be yes, my free hand is balled into a fist tightly. I am wired tight.

"No, nothing I can share at this time."

I hit my leg, three times, hoping she will continue, praying for a better answer. "Okay, I will see you at 10 am," I croak out, my mouth dry, and end the call.

I lay my phone down next to me on the bed.

The call felt wrong. I ball up both my fists before my eyes and breathe in deep. Sucking in air. My body is tense. I unclench my fists, and I run my fingers down my face and sit them in my lap. I try to focus on the fact that the FBI, Agent Scott has a lead. There is something there, a small sliver of something.

Trying to clear the sleep from my head, I check my phone to see if I have other messages. All I see are friends and neighbors asking if I had any updated news on John and Paul.

I delete them all.

I turn the music system on. I need some noise to get out of my head and walk to my closet to change. The song sounds cheerful. It is hard to listen to with my stress reaching nuclear levels and my heart hurting. I want to tell the radio to stop. I yell at the music system to turn off.

How can it be playing happy songs? My mind views the world as the time before we ran out ice and after.

Black and white. Before and after.

I have a tough time choosing clothes. *What does one wear for a meeting with the FBI? Why do I care what Agent Scott thinks?* I am a mess. I almost leave on my Netflix comfy pants, but I reconsider.

I slip on a pair of navy slacks and a gray short-sleeve blouse while standing in the closet. I discard my comfy clothes on the floor, kicking them in the corner. I throw back on my silver sandals, putting my brown hair in a messy bun as I head to the bathroom to wash up and brush my teeth. I am not putting on make-up or adding any extra jewelry today. It's too much work. My phone *bings*. The noise makes me jump. Agent Scott has texted me the address of her office.

In the kitchen, I notice that my new blue mug is still broken on the floor. I make a single cup of coffee from the machine using an old white cup. I look in the refrigerator for some yogurt. Thinking back to yesterday, I realize I have only eaten Oreos and drank some red wine in two days. I grab a spoon from the draw and eat the yogurt in three scoops standing in the kitchen ignoring my broken blue mug on the floor. My coffee is ready, so I take it into the den and turn on the TV. There is no way I am going to the back porch. There is no news of explosion or kidnapping being reported. This makes me angry. I want my family to be found. I want everyone helping. I think about calling someone to complain—the cops, MPs, or maybe Jane and Steve.

I go upstairs and stand at the door to Paul's room. Walking into his room hurts. I sit on the edge of his bed running my hand over his green comforter. Being in his room surrounded by his things kills me.

I close my eyes and I feel like Paul fills the room. Daggers pierce my heart; my breathing is labored, and my eyes are stinging. Tears slide down my face as I look around his room. His discarded algebra book is left open on his desk. I see him in his baseball glove and ball sitting on his nightstand waiting to be picked up. I can almost watch him discard his socks and practice shorts on the floor by his closet as he changed for the pool party. I lay back on his pillow; feeling Paul here is too much. My heart knows Paul here. I cannot hold the pain that is assaulting me. It is heavy and overwhelming. I must go and find Paul. Sunshine filters in the window to remind me that another day is here with no word. I move from his bedroom on shaking legs, taking a moment in the hall to stop and breath. I rest my hand against the wall leaning on the house for support. My body wants to expel the yogurt and coffee I had for breakfast. I feel like I will die in the silence that surrounds me. It is going to swallow me.

Pain floods into me.

I am his mother, and I did not save him. I did not protect him.

I pull my phone out of pocket and I see it has messages. I distract myself through my social media and check email. More friends and John's fellow soldiers check in for updates. I read and delete them all. I am not ready to talk about yesterday to share updates or news. There are no updates on the explosion; the investigators have left me in the dark. I cannot talk about the note I found about Rain. I figure they all know anyway. The guys in the unit share everything. Everyone probably knew about Rain but me. They trust each other with their lives. They knew, they always know. Every man at the party knew of Rain, of what John was up to, and yet, they stood there and smiled at me and thanked me for the party. I am embarrassed, but it flows deeper. I feel used. My anger fills me like a hurricane of thoughts; it whips me up into a storm of emotion, but these feelings are not helping me find my son. To learn what happened to my family, I am going to have to go out there and find the answers for myself. I look back at Paul's room, his things lying there and take a deep breath. I push myself forward.

I walk downstairs, my movements are slow, but steadier than moments before. I aged a thousand years over night. It's 9:15 am, I am ready to go talk to Agent Scott. I grab my keys and Coach purse from the kitchen counter and head out to the garage. It is jarring to see the empty space next to my burgundy Volvo cross-country wagon as I walk around to the driver's door of my car. John's jeep is always parked there. It stays there when he is deployed like a sentinel waiting for his return.

I think of Paul; lately he has been sitting in it. Backing it into the driveway and cleaning it up. Sure, that he was going to be driving it to school when he got his license. I look away from the empty parking space. The pain of the flashes of memories hitting me hard.

I slide into the leather seat of my Volvo. Memories of John flood over me. John had gotten this new car for me as a Christmas present right after we moved here two years ago. I thought it had been too much money, especially with buying the house and Paul's private school tuition payments at the academy, but John had said it was no big deal because he had gotten a bonus. Thinking about it now, I realize it was the last nice present or really any present he had bought me. The last two years had been full of deployments. John had been away much of the time. Paul and I had celebrated most of the recent holidays without John. He had even missed my last two birthdays. I guess I had gotten used to John being gone over the years more than I thought. I had stopped questioning it.

I thought it was all the army. I think about John and Rain.

He kept her note in his pocket, it had been there for a while refolded and close to his heart. I am jealous of the note, of Rain. I bang on the steering wheel trying to remove the hurt from my chest.

I focus on his deception, the cheating. All the receipts I found in John's luggage and then add to that the house remodeling I have been doing, even this new car, I am starting to understand that we have been spending way more money than John could be making in the army. The money may be my key to understand what has happened to my family. To pull out onto the street, I have to drive onto the front yard. I am careful not to disturb the crime scene tape. It is a chilling reminder of what happened here two days ago; fluttering in the breeze. I watch it mocking me in my review mirror as I pull away. Nothing has changed, nothing has been found on Paul and John; we are starting the second day since the event.

Chapter 8

I arrive to my meeting with the FBI at their office off of Sycamore Dairy Road in Fayetteville at 9:30 am on Wednesday. I am early, and I am ready to get answers, who took my family and where they are being held. On television they always seem to pick up the bad guy's trail in a matter of minutes. With all the technology we have in the world, I cannot believe they have nothing, no leads after a day and half. I am under the impression that Agent Scott is the first person to start moving in a direction that will begin to unravel the mystery of where John and Paul have gone, and for the first time since the event, I am optimistic. I take the elevator to the third floor. The music in the elevator is an Elvis tune. I flash to a memory of Paul singing this song last year at his friend's karaoke birthday party. He had been laughing so hard he could barely follow the words on the screen. He kept yelling blue suede shoes as loud as he could. The memory fades as the elevator door opens. I wipe tears from my eyes as I enter the office and ask for Agent Scott. I want my family back.

The receptionist sitting at the front desk has a huge stack of manila folders in front of her. She asks me to take a seat. There are four brown chairs against the wall, and I pick the furthest one from her desk. I pull out my phone and start reading my emails. Another batch of people asking for updates and if I am okay have come through. I scroll and read each one; deleting them. At 10 am, Agent Scott comes out to get me.

"Mrs. Finch, thank you for coming. Please follow me," Agent Scott turns and walks quickly away.

I am not sure what to say. I drop my phone into my purse, rise, and scurry after her into a back room. It is the size of my closet with a long table and three metal chairs. There is a picture of the FBI building in Washington D.C. hanging on the wall. Agent Scott takes a seat at the table and motions for me to take the one opposite her across the table. As I sit down on the metal chair, Agent Scott opens one of those manila folders from the receptionist's desk and starts laying out typed papers in front of her. She removes her smartphone from her pocket and lays it next to the folder. She has a pen in her hand and skims the pages before her, not talking or looking at me. She is wearing another pair of black slacks and a cream-colored long-sleeve blouse today. In her ears are the pearl earrings I noticed on Monday. I can find no watch or other jewelry on her person. Her short, black hair is styled like Kris Jenner, the Kardashians' mother and manager.

I continue to wait for Agent Scott to speak. The room is empty except for the picture and a metal trash can in the corner. The floor and walls could use an update. The place appears as if it has not been remodeled in ten or twenty years. Finally, Agent Scott looks up and slides a piece of paper across the table.

"Stella do you recognize this account at Wells Fargo listed here?" she points to the top of the page.

"No, we bank at USAA. It's all online. John prefers them since they have lower fees and give us a break on our car insurance. I can show you our accounts. I have them all right here on my phone." I know we bank here, but there is nagging doubt about money that is growing.

"Stella, are you sure you have never seen this account? Look again," she taps her pen on the paper. "Your husband, John, has had it for two years. It was opened on 14th street in Washington D.C. It has thirty-two thousand dollars in it. As you can see," she taps her pen on the paper again, "John has been making regular one thousand-dollar deposits into the account for the last two years. No withdrawals have ever been made from this account." Agent Scott sits back in her chair, leaving the paper in front of me as she says, "Look close at the dates and amounts. Where did this money come from, Mrs. Finch?"

I lean forward and inspect the paper. Thirty-two thousand dollars is a substantial amount. "Agent, I don't know anything about this. Maybe John had started a surprise college fund for our son Paul. He is finishing his sophomore year soon…I mean he was…I mean he will be…I mean he is finishing," I take a deep breath. "When Paul is brought home to me, when you find him, he will finish out his sophomore year, tenth grade, and then he will be a junior. That's eleventh grade and one more year and he is off to college. We are hoping for a baseball scholarship, but you know how those go…" I am rambling now, I know, but I cannot stop. My heart is thinking of Paul attending high school, playing baseball. We need to find them. Agent Scott looks at me, collects the paper from the table, and takes her folder. "Agent Scott where is my son? Have you found anything on Paul's whereabouts?" I ask. I feel like we are wasting time. She slides over more papers for me to examine from Wells Fargo.

"Excuse me, Stella, I'll be right back." Getting up, she leaves the room and shuts the door behind her. I sit there, noticing there are no clocks in the room. I pull out my phone. It is already almost 11 am. I try to check the headlines on my social media, but my phone has no signal. I lay my phone on the table and open the photo tab. The last picture of John and Paul at the pool party stares up at me. My breath catches, and my eyes start to water.

Paul is missing, and I am sitting here in this stupid room answering inane questions.

I smack the table with my hand. This is getting me no closer to my son.

I am angry. The room feels warm. I reach down and flutter my blouse letting air in. I hit the side button on my phone and the screen goes black. I start to think about the thirty-two thousand dollars and how that will help Paul go to college. John cheated, we have extra money, and he has an extra secret account.

Thirty minutes later, Agent Scott reenters the room.

"Stella, I apologize. I received a phone call I had to take it. I hope you were okay. Can I get you a bottle of water?" she asks with no sincerity in her voice. I don't feel like she is really sorry for keeping me here.

"Yes, that would be nice," I respond. In the south, we know how to be polite, even when it is killing us. Agent Scott walks back out, this time leaving the door open. I can feel the cold air conditioning from the hallway drifting into the room. She returns in a few minutes with a napkin and a bottle water, handing them to me. I reach for the bottle to open it and realize it is warm.

I guess they do not have a refrigerator here. Agent Scott closes the door stopping the cool air from entering, sits down in her chair, and reopens the file.

"Mrs. Finch are you sure you have never seen this account at Wells Fargo before?" she asks as she moves the paper in front of me again. This time, the account number at the top and the dollar amount in the account are highlighted in yellow. I lean over and look at the paper she is presenting.

"Agent Scott, as I said earlier, we bank at USAA, John handles all the banking and the bills. He always has. He has a degree in math from the University of Miami. That is where we met," I start to stray off topic, the heat and the stress is getting to me. "I was working at the university in the admissions office. A friend had gotten me the job, and he walked in one day and started talking to me about his dreams for the future—graduating college, joining the army, being an officer, traveling the world, and having a family. He was so handsome. I was hooked from the beginning. I helped him sign up for all the classes he needed that day, and he asked me out. The rest, as they say, is history." Again, I am rambling, but I cannot help it. My emotions are high, I am sweating, and I am starting to regret only eating that small yogurt for breakfast. Maybe the coffee, not enough food and lots of questions are making me jittery.

"Mrs. Finch, that is a nice story, but I need to know how John got this money, thirty-two thousand dollars over the last two years," Agent Scott continues. Her tone is accusatory.

I examine the paper in front of me. I have never seen this account.

"I don't know what you want me to tell you. Like I said, John handles all of our money. As I was sitting here waiting for your return, I thought about the amount," I put my hand on the paper, "and what I said about Paul going to college in a few years. I mean, that makes the most sense to me. John is always planning like that. We saved for years for the down payment on our home here in Fayetteville. I am sure that money is John saving money for Paul. He is a good dad," I say, smiling up at Agent Scott. I would have said he was a good guy, but I am not sure anymore. The note from Rain rears its ugly head taunting me. "This is my guess; I do not know about the money. Do you have any information on my son? On where they are? On who took them? You have the entire FBI and all the technology in the world and all you want to do is ask me about these accounts? If you cannot help me, maybe you can find me an Agent who can? You seem to think I am involved somehow. *I am not!*"

I pass her the piece of paper with the bank account information on it. Agent Scott's phone rings, she looks at the caller ID, and as she leaves to answer it, she holds up her finger like she will be a minute, closing the door behind her. About fifteen minutes later, the door opens, and it is the receptionist. I am happy to see someone. I have been trapped in here.

"Mrs. Finch, Agent Scott is going to be awhile. Can I get you a magazine or something?"

"No, I am fine," I reply.

"Great, I am heading to lunch. Please wait here for Agent Scott." She walks off, closing the door.

I think about the thirty-two thousand dollars in the Wells Fargo account and how John could have collected that kind of money. I know we have expenses; I tick them off in my head: The mortgage, household bills, Paul's tuition, and the two car payments. All of that did start to add up each month. I do not know exactly how much John makes as a Major. He never complains about it or says things are tight. In the last two years, we have not talked about money at all. I try to think back to the last time we discussed bills, and that was when we moved to Fayetteville. John had set up all the bills on an automatic payment system through USAA. We do not even get any paper statements to the house anymore. When I shop, I use my USAA Visa credit card and John pays the bill. It sounds so easy, but I now see there is more going on than I was aware. I should have asked more questions of John. I should have paid more attention. I am irate wasting my time with Agent Scott. She is waiting for her *I gotcha* detective moment, but I have nothing to share with her about the account and the money. Since we moved to Fayetteville, I had stopped working. Money has not been tight. John never complains about what I am spending. I was busy fixing up the house and running Paul to all of his practices and games. Before, when we had been stationed elsewhere and we lived on Post, I would get a job working at the hospital or walk-in urgent care clinic helping to check in patients or file records. Since we moved here, that had not been necessary, we had not needed the extra money.

By the time Agent Scott reenters the room, it is after 1 pm, and I am no closer to finding my family than when I got here. My stomach is churning. Agent Scott pulls out new papers.

These new papers are already highlighted. I want to leave, but I am curious; maybe this time Agent Scott has news that will help. I decide to stay.

"Stella, the papers before you are flights your husband has taken to the Middle East over the last two years. What can you tell me about them?" Agent Scott slowly lays three separate flight itineraries in front of me with John's name on them. The first one shows a flight to Amman, Jordan from Raleigh-Durham airport through Atlanta. The second one has highlighted a flight to Rabat, Morocco from Raleigh-Durham through JFK in New York. The third has a longer flight to Aden, Yemen from Raleigh-Durham though Frankfurt, Germany. All of the flights happened in the last year. I scrutinized the flights, dates, and places. The flight to Morocco stands out shouting at me. More proof that John has cheated and that hurts me. I see my marriage differently now. It has been on shaky ground for a while.

"Agent Scott, I am not sure what I can tell you. My husband flies to the Middle East. He tells me he is going on army business. He has been in a long time and I do not question his orders. Sometimes he is gone for months; sometimes a few days. I have gotten used to it. We do not talk about where he is going or what he does there. John is in a special forces' military unit. I am sure you can understand that. I stopped asking questions years ago. I am not sure how I can help you. Maybe you should talk to MP Soto or Detective Johnson; he told me you have all of his phone records," I say, feeling frustrated with her line of questioning and the fact that I realize I really do not know much about my husband anymore. I start to think it has been a long time since John and I had talked about anything of importance. I have been focused on the new house and the remodeling. He has been focused elsewhere. I feel like Agent Scott is mocking me, that she is waiting for me to say something. I realize she is not my friend and she is not going to help me or my family. "I think you know that my husband is having an affair. Are you waiting for me to say it? Is that what you want for me to admit my marriage is not as strong as I thought it was, that we have problems? John is cheating. Okay? Are we done here?" I stand up.

Agent Scott lays down two more pieces of paper in front of me, both with two more flights to places in the Middle East. Agent Scott looks at me and does not acknowledge my outburst. She taps the paper in front of her like a disappointed mother. This agent is sure I am part of this, whatever it is, and I can tell she does not like me. I sit back down. We go on like this, her asking me questions about a dozen flights John took over the last two years and the Wells Fargo bank account, for hours. I do not get answers regarding the whereabouts of John and Paul, but I do get a headache, and I am extremely angry at Agent Scott by the time we are done. I can tell she is not happy with me either. We are at an impasse; I am not helping her create the case she was sure she had, and she is not helping me find my family.

I keep trying to get the answers I need.

"Agent Scott, where is my son? Are you even trying to find him or is this all about intrigue, money and these flights? I feel like you are not even looking. I have been here all day and we are no closer to finding Paul," I bang my hands on the table. I need someone to take me seriously to help me find my son. "I do not think you are helping me. I know you think you have some big case you are making here about John, but I am not sure you are on the right track. Why is Paul's life not important to you?" Agent Scott has no answers for me.

I had spent the day being interrogated; I am not a criminal. I am a victim. I cannot believe this is my life. I have been with Agent Scott at the FBI all day, and we did not accomplish anything that I could tell. My emotions are hanging on by a thread. I feel dark and unforgiven. All today did is shine a light on John's behavior. I do not know my husband.

It is late, after 6 pm, and Agent Scott finally tells me to go home. They would be in touch. I am exhausted, angry, sad, and need something to eat. I feel wrinkled, sweaty and worn out. I am not really feeling up to being in public. Still, I drag myself into the Food Lion grocery store not far from the FBI office and grab a container of sushi from the deli, a bag of Kettle chips, and a new bottle of red wine. The store is bright and crowded. The happy staff and loud store grate on my nerves. I keep my head down like a criminal and walk fast. The smells wafting from the produce aisle upset my empty stomach. I head straight to the self-check-out, not even bothering to swipe my Food Lion MVP card. I am in and out in 5 minutes. I do not want to see anyone I know. I need to get away. I feel like crap.

Stepping out of the automatic doors of the store, I realize that a storm has moved in. The sky above me has darkened, and I move quickly to my Volvo. The clouds are black and swirling. The wind has picked up. The heat of the day has met its match. I do not trouble myself with being careful. My dinner items clank and shift in the plastic grocery bag. The parking lot light turns on next to my car, highlighting it. It is on one of those automatic sensors. The timing makes me glance around the parking lot. I resemble a smuggler on a mission, head down, walking fast. Someone watching would probably think I was an escapee from prison or an insane asylum. I start to run to my car. Agent Scott's questions had taken a lot out of me and my run is more of jog with a skip. My nerves are fried, and my emotions are all over the place. Everything seems hard. I cannot do anything right. It is if I am fighting to free myself from quicksand. My body is not connected to my brain. I stop and fumble with my bag and keys as I get to my car.

I sense someone watching me. The feeling makes the back of my neck shiver.

I slowly look around. The evening smells sweet. As I breathe in, I wrinkle my nose. The yellow parking lot lights are not helping me feel safe. I watch a crumpled white paper bag with a McDonalds arch on it blow across the lot. I stop and wipe a few stray hairs from my face and notice out of the corner of my eye, a Honda parked in the next row pointed towards me. The headlights come on, startling me. I stop like a cat burglar caught by the cops. I do not move, waiting for the wheels to start rolling towards me. I must force myself to get into my car. I am spent, drained from all the questions about John's travel, the money in the accounts; where this was, what that is, and I did not know any of it. It hurts to see that I am a stranger to my own husband's life.

"Silly Stella," I chide myself as I open my car door, watching the Honda pull out of the parking lot. *Someone else is doing a little shopping and trying to get home before the storm.*

I had spent so little time completely alone in the last 15 years, now that I am alone, I think I am being stalked. It was me, Paul and John, or lately just Paul and me. My mind travels to all those late-night movies where the girl, alone at night, is the desperate victim of some psycho. I make a mental note; I need to find something else to watch. The engine of another car sounds loud as it rushes past, maneuvering out of the parking lot. I am on edge. I refuse to turn around and watch it go. I do not want to acknowledge my silly fear of it coming for me like Christine in that Stephen King novel. I have enough on plate. I rest my head on my arms across the steering wheel. I want to cry, but I have no more tears today. I miss my son. I am scared something bad has happened to him and that I will never see him again. I try to move my dark thoughts away and push the positive. John is with him; he will protect his son. Paul is a smart kid; he is going to be okay. I must not give up hope. I try to count my blessings, but I cannot find any.

Suddenly, lightning flashes across the sky. I jump. I sit there looking out the window watching the coming storm clouds. Rain drops begin to fall against the windshield. The big drops hit the window, making a tapping noise like they are knocking to come inside. The storm moves quickly, and the rain falls harder and harder until I cannot see in front me. It is as if the rain drops are trying to break through the glass window to get to me, to touch me, to grab my attention. The rain is working to wake me up. My long stay today with Agent Scott made me recognize that I know nothing about John.

I shiver and sit back in my seat, away from the window. The inside of my car is dark; the tan leather interior feels cold against my skin. The floral air freshener flip-flop hanging from the mirror is heckling me with its happiness. I forcefully rip it down in one fluid motion and throw it in the back seat, not caring where it landed. A bolt of lightning slashes across the sky. The thunder booms, making me jump in my seat, again. It is close. I am near the eye of the storm. The blood starts to pump through my veins, as if I am running a marathon. I can hear my heart beating. I cry out as the next thunderbolt strikes a tree across the parking lot, branches from the tree falling to the ground.

The sound of my own voice in the car startles me. The wind is really starting to whip through the parking lot. Paper and plastic bags fly like a scene from *The Wizard of Oz*. I flinch in my seat, fumble with the keys, and start the car. The engine comes to life instantly. I need to get away from here. I need to go home fast. I throw it into reverse and back out squealing the tires, flying through the parking lot as if I am a fighter pilot on a mission. I am speeding and being reckless to escape from the dangerous storm that is surrounding me. I must move. Hail starts to fall; pelting my Volvo as I speed toward home.

I pull onto my street, my heart racing, and hit the clicker for the garage.

"Damn," I shriek out loud. It is not working. I hit the clicker again for good measure. Nothing happens. The power must be out. Nothing is working in my favor.

"Figures!" I yell at the house. "Cannot catch a break, can you, Stella?" I shout at myself, slamming both my hands on the steering wheel. For some reason, the *Ghostbusters* theme song starts running around in my head, "*Who ya gonna call? Ghostbusters!*" I sing out and start laughing. I am losing it. The stress, my day at the FBI, the worrying about Paul, the revelations about John, it has all been too much. I have gone over the edge to ridiculousness. The yellow caution tape has fallen down and come apart with the storm. The wind has it wrapped around a tree. I see it captured there out of the corner of my eye. As I sit there in the driveway, the rain is still coming down in sheets, making it hard to see my house. Because of the rain and the storm, I cannot tell if the neighbor's power is out as well. I do not see any lights on around me. I look for the police detectives that were supposed to be stationed outside my house and see no one around.

"I am grown woman," I say to the rain. I wipe at the fog accumulating on the window. I sit in the car, glowering at the garage doors. Holding the car door handle with my keys in one hand and grabbing my bag of food and wine from the grocery store in the other, I ready myself. I do not need someone to take care of me or hold my hand. Taking a few deep breaths as if I am preparing to take on a monster, I open the door and race around the car. The rain hits me as I run. I take off with a fast jog toward the front of the house, sliding in my sandals. I am soaked through instantly. Rain pelts me, pushing me faster. Lightning flashes overhead, illuminating the dark sky. *Oh my God, it is crazy out here.* Thunder crashes around me. I jump out of skin.

I leap onto the front porch, shaking myself off like a dog. My sandals are slippery, and my hair is matted to my head. I take the bottle of wine and raise it over my head. I had made it to the front porch. *Hooray, me!*

"I saved the wine!" I shout. I cannot even hear myself over the lightening and rain pelting the house.

I stomp my feet and rail at the gods who have destroyed my life.

I am going nuts.

I am marking my ability to reach my own front door as a success. Turning, I put the key in the lock and open the door. Slowly, my front door swings open. It is pitch black inside. I stand there on the threshold, unsure of what to do next. Like I have a choice. *Am I waiting for someone to offer to go first?* I step in with purpose.

"After you," I say to the wine bottle, thrusting it in front of me.

Besides, if I can save the wine, I figure I can handle the dark. The logic escapes me, but I feel better. I hold the wine in front my body like a sword. As I move into the front hall, I remember I left my phone in my purse in the car. That phone light would have come in handy right about now. *Do I go back to the car in the raging storm to get it? No, I am an adult. I can enter my own house in the dark. I am tired and I need to eat. Hell, I need a drink it has been a long day.* I am probably not thinking clearly at this point; stress, shock, lack of food and all of the questions from Agent Scott. It has been a long day. I need to sit down. I drag myself inside.

I have done stuff like this a million times.

I head straight to the kitchen to find some matches and a candle or a flashlight, and to locate a corkscrew. Conquering the storm and saving the wine makes me feel proud of myself as I strut into the kitchen. I am worn out, and I need to eat. It has been another really long day. I did not get the answers I needed. I am no closer to finding Paul. I need to my son back. I wish this whole thing was over and in the past. I want to feel whole again.

I pull open the junk drawer in the kitchen with one hand to look for the matches, while I am still holding the wine with the other. A strange noise catches my attention. I turn towards the sound. Someone is shuffling papers.

Maybe, I left a window open in the office. I should go shut that before the computer gets soaked.

"John would be so mad at me if I ruined his laptop," I tell the matches I retrieved as I walk through my home. "John," I repeat his name out loud. My heart starts to tell my brain something. I step into the office. A man is standing there, dressed in all black. Lightning flashes in through the window illuminating his shape. Thunder crashes around us.

"*Ahhhhh!*" I scream, lunge forward, and smash the wine bottle over his head reflexively. I am battle ready. Adrenaline is spiking. A man is in my house.

"*Ahhhhh!*" I hit him again. The storm is still raging outside as I attack the man. I am mindlessly swinging the wine bottle at the intruder's head, and for good measure, I fling the book of matches in his face. My actions do not make sense. I am fighting for my survival. It is probably helping that I am a crazy woman, tired, hungry and stressed out from everything that has happened in the last 50 hours. I caught this intruder by surprise; otherwise, I probably would have no chance to survive. I get in a few good blows to his head with the bottle. The man dressed in black sinks to the floor in front of me. My heart is beating so fast I cannot even think. I drop the bottle to the floor. It hits the man in the stomach, rolling onto our tan carpet. The bottle is broken, and wine is spilling out onto the carpet. Or is it blood?

"Oh my *God*!" I yell out. There is a thief, a burglar in my house. I stop.

I hear a crash coming from the bedroom upstairs. Is there more than one intruder? I run to grab the phone on John's desk.

It is dead.

"Damn, power outage!" I whisper at the phone. I see papers scattered across the desk and on the floor. The window is open in front of me and rain is splattering into the room. The room is torn apart. There are even holes in the wall. I feel like the storm has let this danger into my home. I run back through the house towards the front door to retrieve my phone from the Volvo. Another man dressed in black comes barreling out of nowhere, startling me. He is coming towards me. He has a gun pointed at me. I try to turn around, but my wet feet in my wet sandals were not cooperating. Instead, I slip and hit the framed pictures on the wall. The pictures clatter to the floor, the glass frames cracking and shattering. The intruder continues forward menacingly, his large gun pointed at my face. All I can see is the barrel of the gun.

"*Stop!*" I scream and throw my hands in front of me. My next thought is that I need a gun or a weapon. I spot the broken glass on the floor and reach down to grab it. My heart is thumping in my chest. My thoughts fire rapidly through my brain. I scoot away from the intruder. He very deliberately raises his voice above my yelling.

"Where are the guns?" he demands in a strong Middle-Eastern accent.

"I don't know what you are talking about!" I shout at him. "Go, please! Go away!"

I throw the pieces of glass at the intruder, and he fire his gun as the glass shards collide with his face. The bullet narrowly misses me.

"Where are the guns, Colonel wife?" he shouts at me. The gunfire momentarily deafens me, like a bomb going off. I can no longer hear the storm raging outside or the chaos in my house. Everything seems to be moving in slow motion.

I scramble for answers. I need to get away from this guy. Lightning and thunder shake the house. The storm is raging outside. It comes to me out of the blue that John kept a gun in the closet in our bedroom. I don't think that is the gun this guy is talking about. He called John a colonel. John is a major? The craziness of the situation makes my thoughts spiral in weird directions.

The intruder shouts again, "Guns, Now! Where are my guns? We paid."

I shake my head at him. He reaches for my arm, but since I am soaked from the rain, I slide away; his black gloves cannot grip me. I don't know what he is talking about. I back away, trying to turn the corner towards the front door, sliding in my wet sandals on the wood floor. I turn and look down the hall behind me. Unbelievably, I focus on another man, a third man coming through the front door, who is pointing a gun right at me. *What the hell!* A week ago, I was planning a pool party and now I am starring in my own horror movie. I need to get out of this house. Where were all these men with guns coming from at six o'clock on a Wednesday? I live in a sleepy neighborhood that is usually so quiet. I grab my blouse and try to pull it up to protect myself, like it is made of armor. I am scared; if I can't see the bullet coming, maybe it won't come.

None of this made sense. The third man, now in front of me, steps around me and, in an instant, grabs my arm and bodily pushes me behind him, around the corner and away from the man demanding guns. I slip and fall to the floor, crashing against the wall from the momentum. Red wine or blood cover my arms and hands. I try to pick myself up off the floor.

The rain is still falling outside, beating on the roof, trying to get in and join the melee. Lightning flashes across the windows. Smoke reaches me as I take in ragged breaths. Gun shots ring out. One, two, three thunder claps cover the noise like a loud drum solo, stealing the show. The house shakes. *Or am I shaking?* The man with the gun pulls me up against him and off the floor like I am a rag doll dragging me towards the door. He is much taller than me. Behind him, the second intruder lay unmoving on the hallway floor, bullet holes peppering his head and chest. *There are two dead bodies in my home.* My thoughts scatter.

I try to wrench my arm away from the tall, dark-skinned man holding the gun. He will not let go. He does not even look back toward the house or at me. He is pulling me to the beige Honda in my driveway. I must save myself. I struggle harder against his grip, my sandals slipping around my feet in the wet grass. Wind whips my long, brown hair into my face. I am able to slip free a little from his tight grasp as the rain continues to fall on us. He stops then, turning around to look at me, still holding his gun.

I take stock of my kidnapper; he is taller than me but shorter than John. He has short, black hair, shaved close, military style, and a solid muscular build. His arms are as big as my thighs. He is enormous. He is not a guy who gets messed with often. His hazel eyes look at me with an intense emotion I cannot name, as we stand there in my front yard, getting soaked by the rain. My chest is heaving from fear, from running, and from killing the intruder with the wine bottle. My flight and fight responses have really kicked in. The man with the gun seems to think of something and half-way smiles as if he thought of an inside joke. His smile changes his face, and he looks friendly; kind almost.

He says, "Come with me if you want to live!"

"*Ha!*" I shout over the rain. "What are you, the Terminator? You don't look like Arnold Schwarzenegger." This really wasn't the time to be joking, but I can't help it. Something about the stranger makes me want to engage.

"No, not a Terminator!" he shouts back. "But I have always wanted to use that line." He reaches for my hand again, closing the space between us. His demeanor is gentle now. His touch has changed. My flight or fight response is still kicking in and I am still trying to get away.

"No way! I am not going with you!" I yell above the storm, trying to free my hand. My hair is plastered to my face, making it hard to see. Light is now spilling out of my house from the front windows across the lawn. I swing my other arm trying to hit the man in the face. He easily grabs my hand bringing it down and holding it between us with his other hand still holding the gun he reaches behind me pulling me closer. There are mere inches separating us.

"Yes, Stella, you are. I can help you, let me help you," he says softly, staring directly into my eyes. He reaches up and moves a piece of my hair that is fallen forward over my eye and places it behind my ear. The thought, *how does he know my name?* bounces into my head. "Stella, we need to go. Let me help you find your family."

Chapter 9

The rain is beginning to soften as the storm passes. The wind has stopped, and the lightening has moved on. He straightens his shoulders, and gently squeezes my shoulder as he lets me think about what he has said. I want to trust him. I must be brave. Paul is still out there, and I will do anything to get him back. I would trade his life for mine.

"I am with the CIA," he flips open a badge. "You are in danger. You have been. You are a good woman who has been dealt a shitty hand. Let me help you." Somehow, during his little speech, he is leading me to the car. He is not waiting for my answer. He is holding his side. "Stella, I am going to need you to drive. You can do this. I trust you."

He carefully ushers me to the driver's seat of his car. I cannot remember the last time John opened my car door. He helps me into the car and carefully closes the door, leaving me alone in the deafening silence. My mind is buzzing, and as I silently sink into the leather seat, images come to me in flashes. The guy across the street the day John and Paul went missing. Him again, earlier tonight at the grocery store. Arriving home and the garage door not opening. Saving the bottle of wine and smashing it over the intruder's head. *I killed him; I killed a man—oh my God!* Panicking and running through the house. The thick smell of smoke. The dead man shot in my front hallway. The images are disjointed and scary.

My breathing accelerates. I clench my hands in front of me. I am having a mini panic attack. There are dead men in my home. *I killed a person.* The intruder's words are on repeat in my brain. *Guns. He wanted guns. He paid for guns.*

I try to make sense of the intruder's demands. I look up from my hands and across my beautifully manicured lawn. Too much light is spilling out of the windows. The smoke I smelled—*the intruders must have started a fire.* The realization hits me in the chest. I hug my forearms across my chest and squeeze my eyes shut, willing this all to go away, shaking my head hoping to wipe away the events of the last fifteen minutes.

I instinctively reach over to buckle my seat belt. I slowly pull out of my driveway and onto the road. The CIA agent sitting next to me starts to buckle his seat belt as well.

I take a deep breath. The potent air freshener hanging from the rearview mirror is trying, unsuccessfully, to mask the smell of old gym socks. Countless questions race through my mind.

John, what have you done? I am starting to understand that John may not be who I thought he was and that all of this is his fault. The money, the trips away, those men wanting guns—I start to connect the dots. All roads lead to John. I take a deep breath and try not to freak out.

Abruptly, I remember the light coming from the front window of my house.

"Excuse me," I urgently break the silence. "Why was there a light in the windows when we left? The house had no power. What did they do?" My voice sounds shaky and unfamiliar.

The stranger responds slowly.

"Your home was on fire," he clarifies. "It looks like it was started upstairs, maybe to cover their tracks."

The fire seems like a fitting ending to the events of the last three days. It marks the disaster that is now my life.

Oh, John, what have you gotten us into?

I sigh. There are no tears or strong words left. I cannot feel anything about what I am leaving behind in Fayetteville. This fire concludes the chaos that the original Jeep fire launched on Monday, making a clean sweep of everything I had once cared for and turning it into a mound of ash. It is now Wednesday evening, and whatever John is involved in has destroyed my life. I bang my hands on the steering wheel.

My husband is not one of the good guys, like I thought. *He is a bad guy, a criminal.* Good guys do not exchange guns for money. Good guys do not keep secret bank accounts. Good guys do not have affairs.

The rain continues to fall lightly. I watch the silent rain drops fall on the car window as we pass familiar stores and restaurants, leaving the downtown area. I am drained, bone tired. I remember that I have not really eaten today. A cup of yogurt, a cup of coffee, and a warm bottle of water these sound like an impossible Hollywood diet fad. Those three things would be the spam headline,

Yogurt Coffee Water Diet, on your Facebook page leading you into a virus that crashes your computer and probably would kill you if you tried it. Not eating seems like such a minor problem on top of everything else that is happening to me. I cannot focus on myself. I must be a mom first.

I continue to drive. My thoughts are on Paul. I need to find my son. This CIA agent could be the key to helping me. I become resolute. In these quiet moments in the car, when I am breathing in and out and the sound of my breath fills the space, I know—down in my soul—that Paul is still alive out there. The terrible things that have happened don't matter; I feel that he knows I am here, looking for him. I say a silent prayer, hoping that Paul is safe. I need my boy to be okay. It has been 51 hours since Paul and John went missing. What else could possibly go wrong? I have already lost my family and my home.

Chapter 10

As we leave Fayetteville, pulling onto the I-95 North, the pine trees along the side of the road quietly watch us depart. The road is empty; the rain has stopped. The lights from the highway shine off of the wet road and the world outside looks new where the light hits it. I'm reminded of how little I drive at night.

A few semi-trucks are heading down the highway in the opposite direction. The car is quiet; the late evening has grown silent around us, but my brain has not. As I drive, I think about my meeting with the FBI. The more I review the facts, the more I can admit to myself that John is doing something that is criminal. The money, the flights, the intruders in my home searching for guns—this all adds up to some serious stuff. Someone does not need to watch James Bond to figure this out. He has done more than cheat on me. I realize I need to start asking questions.

"Umm, what's your name? You already know mine, so it's only fair that I know yours," I ask.

"Chris," he says, not taking his eyes off the road ahead of us.

"You mean like Christopher Columbus; the one who sailed the ocean blue in 1492?" I ask.

"Yes, I guess if that's what you want to think," Chris replies.

"Where are we headed?" I nod to the windshield. "Besides north."

"Washington D.C.," he says; as if that explains everything.

I look Chris over, trying to figure out what to ask next. I notice that he is bleeding down his side. His shirt and the seat are covered in blood.

"You're really bleeding a lot," I gasp. "I can help you. Let's pull over."

"No," He growls, keeping his eyes on the road. "I will be fine, it will stop. We need to keep moving. Those men were not alone in this. We need to get you somewhere safe."

"Why? I can help. Do you want to bleed out, right here, right now?" I am a little irritated. Not eating all day and killing a guy has made me cranky.

"What is your problem? You can save my life, but I cannot save yours? Stop acting all invincible, warrior man. I am pulling over at the next rest stop. The least I can do after you saved me is help you." I gently touch his forearm. "Unless you are some kind of Terminator that can heal yourself," I say, more sarcastically than I intend.

Chris does not respond to my joke. I nervously tap my hand on my leg.

We pass a green highway sign that states the next rest stop is 10 miles ahead.

Maybe…they have a snack machine. If I eat, I won't be as cranky.

I suddenly realize that I left my purse back in my car. My phone, too.

Who am I going to call? I have no family. I should call the police, tell Detective Johnson or MP Soto that there are two dead guys in my house, I have been abducted—no, rescued—by a CIA terminator dude.

Who would believe me? I cannot call Agent Scott who questioned me all day. She is not on my side. Agent Scott thinks I am criminal working with John. She is sure she has a big money case.

Wow, I left everything back there; that is so unlike me. What am I saying? It isn't normal for me flee for my life after being attacked. All of this is past crazy.

I laugh out loud. Chris looks at me strangely. "I am sorry. I am going a little crazy I think."

I am on the verge of falling apart. I need to stop thinking so much about all of the who, what, and why of what happened back at my home. Who would have thought, less than three days ago, that I would be here? I was leading the all-American life.

"Stella, you are doing great. Go ahead and pull in. You are right. Let's get me cleaned up. I know you are going through a lot and I should not make things harder on you." Chris smiles at me.

I pull into the rest stop. The rain has stopped; the storm has moved on. The head lights from the cars pulling in and out make everything brighter as the sun sets behind us. Chris gets out of the car without a word and grabs a duffel bag from the trunk. I get out, stretch, and tilt my head up to the sky, looking for answers. There is a slight chill in the air, accentuated by my damp clothes. I am exhausted and still shaken as I follow Chris up towards the bathrooms. I watch everything around us, waiting for another boogeyman to jump out at me.

Chris enters the ladies' bathroom room with a quick look back at me, expecting me to follow like a good puppy. *Thank God. I really do not want to go into the men's room.* Ladies bathrooms are usually much cleaner.

"Okay," I say. "What do you have in the bag?"

He pulls his shirt over his head to reveal a chiseled torso with dried blood cutting down the right side. The bleeding had stopped. I take the wet shirt from his hand and run it under the tap.

"Stella, none of this is your fault. I am sorry about your home. It seemed like a nice place. From what I understand, you have spent a lot of time fixing it up over the last few years. I will help you find your family. Thanks for driving us here and taking care of me like this," Chris says as I bend over and clean his side.

"Cleaning up your wound, is the least I could do since you saved me from those crazy intruders at my house. All I want to do is return to a normal life and find my son...so...thank you," I reply. I am not sure what to say at this point. I will take any help I can get.

Chris does not move; his calmness is starting to help me. His quiet demeanor is like a safe harbor in the storm. I feel myself connecting with it and feeling less scattered. I clean the dried blood until a straight, horizontal gash is revealed under his arm near his rib cage. It does not look that bad for all the blood on his shirt.

"I can understand that, I would do anything to have my family back," Chris whispers. I am not sure I heard him correctly.

"Well, you won't die," I say, still looking at the wound.

Chris lets out a barely audible grunt that could have been a laugh. He reaches in the bag and pulls out a brown leather travel kit. Inside is a small, airplane-sized bottle of vodka. He hands it to me.

I pour it on the wound, looking up to gauge his reaction. His face is stone, and his body is still. His breathing is even.

"Maybe you are the Terminator," I say up at him. "A robot sent from the future to save me." I laugh a little at my joke.

Chris's reply is to sternly shake his head.

His quiet words fill the poorly lit bathroom; the line of sinks and white stall doors absorb his powerful words. The place smells like Pine Sol and bleach. I look at him. I can see Chris is sad.

"So, is there a Mrs. Chris Terminator and family out there waiting for you to come home?" I ask making conversation. I think he is going to say more. Instead, he grabs a clean T-shirt out of the duffel bag and walks out, taking his things and leaving me alone.

I look in the mirror above the sink and run my hands through my hair. It's still damp from the rain. I shake my head.

I wash my hands and wipe myself off quickly and hurry after Chris into the rest stop parking lot. A few cars are scattered around. An older man in a Disney World T-shirt and jean shorts is walking up the path towards me. He has on the old-man uniform of socks and slip-on sandals that at any other time would have made me smile. After my week, I do not trust anyone. Even harmless looking old men raise my hackles.

I cut across the damp grass to avoid him, slipping a little in my haste. I curse my damn sandals under my breath.

I shout towards Chris, "Stop! Wait up!"

He is already standing by the car. He stops what he was doing and looks at me. The old man continues walking towards the restrooms.

"Did you know John and Paul were going to be kidnapped?" the words rush out of my mouth as I approach the Honda.

Chris looks me straight in the eye. I can feel the tension even though we are still a few feet apart. He presses his lips together and opens his mouth. I can tell he is deciding what to say. A minivan packed full of a family backs out next to us and starts towards me. Chris grabs my arm and pulls me to him like I weigh nothing.

"*No*, I did not know about that," he responds setting me down in front of him.

"Get out of the middle of the road," he grunts. "Are you trying to get yourself killed?"

I am pressed to his chest. The impact of our two bodies colliding startles me. I raise my hand to his shoulder to steady myself.

The twenty seconds we stand, pressed together, feels longer. He looks like he is trying to figure out what comes next. I have a sudden, irrational urge to lay my head on his shoulder and hug him. Our breath mingles in the night air.

Abruptly, as if he could read my mind, he lets go of my arm and turns. He jumps into the car and slams the door. I stand there, stunned by his abrupt departure.

I walk around the back of the car and follow his lead, slamming my car door, and reach over to turn on the radio.

Chris pulls out onto the highway as a sad country song plays on the radio. I lean against the window; slow tears roll down my face. I am sick of the drama and the chaos. I want to be home with my family. A sad country song continues to play.

I wipe my face and stare out the window into the night, watching the passing pine trees on the side of the road. I inspect my hands playing with my wedding ring reflecting on John and Rain. I am more than exhausted, my whole-body aches from the inside out. My home is gone, burned. My son and my husband are still missing. I feel useless.

"Stella, why don't you tell me about your son, Paul? Sometimes it helps if you talk about things. I have been told," Chris says as he continues to drive us down I-95.

"Paul is a boy becoming a teenager. He is growing up. Over the last year he shot up and grew, oh my god. He got so tall. He likes to make me laugh by telling me silly jokes. We spend a lot of time together just the two of us since John is always deployed…gone. He likes all of those racing car movies; *Fast and Furious* I think they are called," I cannot stop talking about Paul; all of my mom pride is pouring out of me. "He is smart, he gets really good grades in math and science. He loves to experiment and do all those science projects. Which is funny, because I always hated those when I was in school. I guess he loves baseball the most out of anything and he is good. I mean like really good at it. That worries me sometimes because I feel like he won't look at other options for his life. 'Cause he is a smart kid he can do so much. I am such a helicopter mom; I worry about everything and nothing." I start to laugh at myself. The laughter feels good. Talking about Paul helped; I feel less stressed out. "Hey, thank you for that, talking about Paul did help. You were right."

"No problem. I liked hearing about him. I can tell he means the world to you. Don't worry, I will find a way to help you get your son back."

I feel like Chris's words are a bond between us. The talking has somehow brought us closer. I still fill all smashed through to my soul and twisted my insides, all spiky, jagged, and uncomfortable, but there is hope there, too. A small glimmer of hopefulness and faith has taken root.

Sitting in silence, images of my new, beautiful home burning to the ground taunt me as the miles roll beneath us. Losing my home hurts, but not as much as John's secrets with Rain, not as much as missing my son Paul. A drop of water runs down the window and I follow it with my finger as it slips away. I do not want to talk to Chris about John cheating.

I curl tighter into myself, trying to protect myself from my new harsh reality full of explosions, intruders and fires. The Honda's leather seat feels cold against my skin. Closing my eyes, I try to block it all out.

I need a few minutes of sanity. I look over to Chris. I am grateful to him for saving my life tonight. I made the right decision to trust him. I watch Chris drive.

Chris looks over at me.

"I had a wife, a Mrs. Chris. We were expecting our first child, a little girl. My wife was killed last year in a car accident while I was away from home on assignment. I did not even know for a few weeks that she was gone. The CIA did not want to interrupt the job I was on, undercover. Her parents had her funeral without me. I would do anything to get them back," his words fill the silence.

"I am sorry," I whisper as I put my hand over his.

He had a wife; a family and they are gone. I feel closer to Chris. I cannot imagine the pain of hearing you lost your family weeks after they were gone. I do not think I would forgive the CIA for keeping that information from me.

I hold Chris's hand tighter. I feel like he knows my pain, the pain of losing everything. In a strange way, I feel like I have made a new friend, like we are in this together.

Chapter 11

Chris's words sit with me, and I think about what he said. He has been watching over me this last month, like a guardian angel. I know, without Chris, the intruders would have probably killed me looking for John's guns. I can only be thankful that he was there for whatever reason that brought Chris here. I look over at him and smile. Something has changed between Chris and me; his revelation has changed us.

I spot a McDonalds down the road. I inspect a dark stain on my navy pant leg, touching it with my hand.

"Hey," I ask, "can we pull into McD's? I need to clean-up a bit more and I could use something to eat." I had not eaten anything since this morning's cup of yogurt. It is now late Wednesday night.

Chris looks over at me like I have two heads.

"What! A lady can't get hungry? Even people who are being attacked by criminals need to eat once in a while." I give him my most serious face. I will get my way in this. "Besides, who is going to look for us at a fast-food restaurant. It does not sound like a stop in any spy movie I have ever seen." I realize I also need to use the bathroom and the more I think about it, the more I have to go.

"Fine," Chris sighs. "We'll stop for five minutes. No more than that."

"Great, you can get me a Quarter Pounder with cheese combo meal, with a large diet Coke to go." I smile up at him. Chris looks shocked that I gave him my order.

"Okay," Chris replies, rubbing his hand across his jawline. He pulls in the driveway of McDonalds and parks in the back. I jump out.

"Meet you inside," I call as I run for the ladies' room.

"Wait," Chris calls after me, but I am already gone.

Ten minutes later, I walk out of the McDonalds; fed and feeling more human than I have in the last few hours. I had washed my face and fixed my hair into a reasonable-looking ponytail. It was hard to tell that a few hours ago, I had killed someone with a wine bottle and watched another guy get shot, and that I am now on the run.

"Is your life always this crazy?" I wave my hand in front of me as we settle back in the car. "I mean, as a CIA agent or whatever, you must meet people like me every day."

Chris looks over at me and shakes his head. I start to admire his profile. I stop smiling, suddenly angry at myself for admiring Chris. The past few days slam into me. Paul is still gone, and I have no answers. Chris should be the farthest thing from my mind. As we drive north into the city, I pray for Paul's safe return. I need to figure out why the intruders were looking for guns in my home or I am never going to feel safe again.

We travel along the highway into D.C. and cross into the city near the Lincoln Memorial. The city is asleep. I sit back and close my eyes, thinking of the time that John, Paul and I had visited the monuments as a family. It feels like forever ago. Paul was a small child, holding my hand and chasing the birds in the park. We were a happy family, out doing the tourist thing in D.C. I turn to tell Chris about the last time I was here with my family. He interrupts me with his new plan.

"Stella, I am going drop you around the corner at this hotel where a friend of mine works. I need to go to the office and talk to a few people, and you cannot be with me. It is important to me that you are safe." He still has both hands on the steering wheel.

"What?" I cannot comprehend his plan. "After all this, you are leaving me?"

"No, *no, no*, I am not leaving you. I am protecting you. I am going to help you find your son," Chris replies softly, his words filling the car. "I need to stash you someplace safe, someplace no one will think to look, while I find out a few things. No one will look for you at a high-end hotel. Airports, malls, out here at the Smithsonian, these places have surveillance cameras. If someone is looking for us, they can spot you there. This hotel I know has no cameras. A lot of important people stay there. They make it a point to protect their guests' privacy," he clarifies.

"Okay, I get it. I need you to find out more information about what happened at my house. To see if they are any updates on John and Paul," I respond cautiously. I feel like I am still splattered with wine and blood, even though I had washed up at the McDonalds. I could probably use a shower. Most importantly, I need Chris's help with finding my family.

"I need to talk to some people, and I need to know you are safe. Here," Chris says as he hands me a wad of cash, "down the street in the circle is the Mandarin Oriental. It is across from the Starbucks; walk up to the desk and ask for Lori. Say that Chris sent you. Meet me back in the lobby at 8 am, tomorrow, Thursday; that's in a little over nine hours from now. I know you can do this. You are stronger than you know, Stella. I am not going to desert you. I promise." I listen to Chris's instructions. He saved my life once before. I try to reason with myself that I can trust him.

Chris drives down the street a few more blocks before he pulls over to the curb. Unexpectedly, Chris reaches over and squeezes my hand, then reaches across me to open my door. The contact is reassuring. Still, I feel like a small child in trouble as I get out of the car. I look back and stand there, watching him pull away. I am alone again, but this time in a new city.

Chris's faith in me to stay safe has given me courage. I know I can do this. I feel like we are team. It is strange that I have only known him a short time but that he is a big part of my thoughts. I hope he can find more information on where John and Paul have been taken.

I turn and walk into the hotel, careful to keep my head down and my feet on the right path. I should be scared or worried, but at this point, I am too wiped out. I focus on getting my feet to take me to the hotel.

The hotel is gorgeous with gleaming, tan, marble floors and dark wood columns. The place is made to be calm; I need calm. It smells like fresh, exotic flowers and polished wood. I walk to the center of the lobby with my eyes fixed on the design on the floor. I walk up to a beautiful flower arrangement on a table in the middle of the vast room. I study my surroundings, admiring the way the light filters across the ceiling. I try to look nonchalant, like I had been out for a walk and was returning to my room. I feel out of place and I cannot stop talking to myself.

Be calm, Stella, be cool! Ask for Lori, you can do this. In the lobby, Frank Sinatra's song *Someone to Watch Over Me* is playing softly. I focus. To my right is the front desk.

I am suddenly very aware that I need a long, hot shower. I walk up to the front desk with my head held high, summoning every ounce of energy I can muster to pull this off. *I can do this. Be calm, Stella.*

I want the employees to think that I am a regular guest of the hotel, that coming in at 3 am with no luggage is a normal, everyday occurrence for me. A blonde, skinny desk clerk wearing too much make-up and a black uniform shirt with a high notched Japanese collar greets me at the desk.

"Hello, welcome to the Mandarin," she croons in a smooth, sexy voice. "How may we be of service to you today?" She does not seem to know how to smile.

I look her in the eye and say nonchalantly, "Hello, I would like to speak to Lori."

The attendant responds with a tight smile, "Of course, one moment," and walks to the back.

A tall woman walks out to the desk and greets me quietly, "Hello, I am Lori. How can I assist you?"

"Hello," I repeat to her without looking up. "Chris sent me."

Lori starts to type on the computer.

"That will be three hundred dollars for the night," she states without looking up from her computer.

I reach in my pocket and count out three hundred dollars from the bills Chris handed me when I left the car. I push them across the counter.

Lori hands me a set of room keys in a little folder. I walk away, amazed at what transpired; how easy it is and how weird it was to check into this hotel like a criminal with no name and credit card.

I take the elevator to my hotel room and slip inside. I turn the TV to the national news, not sure if I am hoping or dreading to see anything about my life flash across the screen. I look at the hotel room phone and think about calling Colonel Steve's house and speaking to Jane. I realize that without my iPhone, I do not know their phone number. I don't know how to contact anyone that might be of help—not Detective Johnson, MP Soto, or even Chris. Hell, I don't even know Chris's last name. I look around the room and think of Paul. I wonder where he is and if he is safe. I feel guilty that I am here in this nice hotel room. Sadness overcomes me, and I sit on the bed. There is nothing I can do here for Paul. I inspect the stains on my slacks. I pick at the dried red stain. It takes me awhile to focus. I am lost in my thoughts. Finally, I decide the first order of business is to scrub away all signs of my fight with the intruders at my home. It takes all my energy to get up from the bed. I slide off my sandals. I realize I need to wash my clothes too. I turn on the shower and step in fully clothed. Standing under the spray I try to wash it all away. I hang on to Chris's words that this is not my fault. Slowly, I unzip my slacks and let them fall.

One by one I remove my clothes dropping them to the floor to puddle around me. I reach for the small bottle of body soap and poor it into my hands. I lather my body, trying to clean away all the bad. As I finish, I sit down pushing my clothes towards the corner of the shower. I let the hot water stream over me as I walk through the events of the last few hours from the intruders, to my home in flames, to my road trip with Chris. I turn off the shower and hang up my clothes to dry. With my last bit of energy, I crawl into the large comfortable bed with thoughts of John, Chris and Paul tumbling around in my head.

Eight hours later, I am walking back through the lobby feeling better about myself. I am showered, rested and redressed in my semi-clean damp clothes from yesterday. As I walk through lobby, I notice a boutique selling women's clothes. I glance down at my outfit. I had picked this out to meet with Agent Scott yesterday. She was such a witch and then the intruders—I feel like this outfit has bad mojo. I had scrubbed the stains in the hotel room and hung it up to dry, but I still looked a mess. I step into the store and pick up a pair of tan Capri pants, a springy blue top, and some strappy wedge sandals that the store has on display together. I march toward the dressing room. New clothes that fit me are something I can control. There has been very little I can control in my life over the last few days.

Two minutes later, I am staring at myself in the mirror, dressed in my new outfit. I have dropped some weight this week. I turn around and notice that even my butt looks decent in these pants. I pull off all the tags, something I would have never done before. I fold yesterday's clothes into a little pile and pick them up with the tags.

I strut to the counter with a new attitude. The shop clerk, who looks like an old church grandma, eyes me over her reading spectacles and skeptically asks if I am ready to check out.

"Yes," I say and drop the handful of clothing tags onto the counter. They flutter down like a pile of butterflies. "I am going to wear my new outfit out," I inform her cockily, as if I am a small child buying a new pair of tennis shoes for the first day of school. I do not care. I glower at the woman behind the counter, daring her to say something to me. She gives me a bag for my worn clothes.

I am going to get through this alive and find my son. Rest and a shower have made me stronger. I walk straight out into the high-end lobby, swinging my bag like I own the place, and bump right into Chris. Once again, our bodies connect, and for a moment I can feel my heartbeat. As he moves to my side, I smile at him.

He has showered and changed his clothes as well.

"Do you have any news on John and Paul or the intruders asking for guns at my home?" Chris looks at me for a moment. I can see he is thinking about what to say or maybe he is confused by my new outfit.

"Good news, I do have a lead on the intruders looking for guns. We are going to meet an old friend. I think he may know what is going on, but he will only talk in person. The bad news is we are pretty sure John and Paul were taken out of the country on a private jet. We have tracked their movements out of Fayetteville and to a private airstrip in Virginia." Chris watches me for a reaction. I try not to break down at the mention of my family. "Stella, you have been very strong through all of this," he finishes.

I am grateful for news of Paul. My mind travels to all the places he could be with a plane leaving the country, he could be anywhere. Joining forces with Chris is a step in the right direction. I am excited to finally have a lead. I am tired of waiting on everyone else to solve this.

I am going to find my family. The excitement of moving towards a lead almost has me giddy as I grab Chris's hand as we walk out of the hotel. I am happy Chris has come back for me. And we have a new plan to figure out what is going on. It is going to be a good day. I feel like we are on the right path. I walk out of the hotel with hope in my heart for the first time in days.

Chapter 12

Walking through the city, I catch myself watching Chris, admiring his profile. I try to think about John and our life together, about how I should be angry at him for Rain. Willing my brain to switch gears and go back to solving the problem of John's guns in our home. My mind switches to focus on the note I found in his pocket. The name with the cute heart drawn at the bottom, Rain. I begin to get a clearer picture of why John had been so hard to talk to lately. Why we had not had sex in a long time. I try to think about John's actions without my heartache getting in the way. I need to look at the facts if I am going to find Paul. Chris's lead, that they left Virginia in a private jet, gives me some hope that they are still alive.

It is hard for me to believe that John is putting our troops, our soldiers, his friends, in danger. John was always a very good soldier. Why would he do these things, money or love of this Rain woman it is hard for me to accept.

John is a bad guy.

It hurts me to admit it. Our marriage had not been good for a while, but I did not want to give up on it.

I am married to a criminal who sells guns to other criminals.

I picture the intruders in my house shoving the gun in my face. My stomach hurts as I remember the terror of this moment. I wipe my sweaty palms on my capri pants as I close my eyes and try to wipe it all from my mind.

With everything I am learning about John, this is still very hard for me to swallow that he would betray his country. The proof though seems irrefutable; there were intruders tearing apart our home looking for guns. One thought pops into my head, *the man with the gun, he called John a colonel. John is a major.*

There is a hole in this story, I am sure. There is something I do not know yet. Somehow, I know deep down, there is more going on with John. There is more to his disappearance than anyone had been able to explain to me. The timeline of the explosion—or the event, as the investigating team called it—is starting to be filled in with little pieces of the puzzle. Still, I am missing something. I need more answers. I hope Chris's friend has the answers. It's already Thursday and I feel like I am running out of time.

I am failing my son. This thought rocks through my body. How can I be happy when Paul is missing? I must focus, I reach for my heart necklace that Paul gave me for Mother's Day last year and hold on tight. Finding answers is where I start on the right path, no more waiting around. Chris takes my hand into his and we weave through the tourists. We look like a couple on vacation. Chris explains that this man is going to meet us at the Hay Adams Hotel by the White House.

"I feel like this guy is going to give us the lead that breaks this case open. Helping us to find your family and what is really go on," he says as we walk down the street.

"Where do you know this guy from? Is he really your friend or a CIA contact?" I ask, nervous about being out surrounded by all these people. I see my intruders everywhere lurking in the shadows ready to attack.

"He is a CIA friend; he was an informant on a case I worked awhile back. But I think we can trust him."

I mull over this and I start to wonder if the investigation team has gone by my house and tried to reach me. I wonder what Agent Scott will think of my burned-up home. Panic starts to creep up on me. I look over at Chris and calm comes in. Together, I know we are going to solve this.

Hopefully, Chris's friend will help. The crowds of people around us are making me uneasy. I am searching for bad guys behind every tree. It is a long walk through the city, and I am wishing we had taken Chris's car. He had tried to explain that with all the one-way streets, traffic and parking that walking would be faster. I am already regretting my new shoes.

A handsome, older doorman in a smart uniform opens the door for us as we enter. He smiles and inquires if we are checking in.

"Hello, Welcome to the Hay Adams," he espouses. I notice more doormen stand at the ready to help guests, open doors, or hail cabs. This is a nice hotel. I wonder what John and Rain's hotel was like in Morocco. Was it as nice as this one? Jealousy springs up inside me. John's affair sneaks into my heart and starts to eat at me. Curling around me and filling me full of wrath and emotion. I dwell on these emotions. I am watching every couple I spot like they are John and Rain.

I run my hand through my hair and take a deep breath. We decide to take a seat on the lobby couches and wait for his friend. The area is decorated with chandeliers. The lobby is busy with families this afternoon. School is out, and people are taking advantage of the summer break to see the sites. The families swirling around me make me sad. I see Paul everywhere. I think about how much time we spend together with John gone all of the time. It has really been the two of us. Paul is doing well in high school; he likes his classes. In the evenings, we talk about his homework and even the girl he is interested in. I reflect on our taco Tuesdays and pizza Fridays. How we argue over wing sauces. Paul likes them super spicy. I can picture him laughing at me in the kitchen as I burn my mouth on his favorites. I remember our last argument when he wanted to adopt a rescue we saw at an event outside the mall. I said no, we need to have John home and make it a family decision. Paul was so mad at me. I would give anything to get him that dog today. We sit in the lobby for hours waiting. I am about to give up all hope.

Out of the corner of my eye, I see a short, Italian-looking man, wearing tan slacks and a crisp white, short-sleeve dress shirt, enter the lobby. He turns, glances around, smiles, and heads toward us. He has a big, wide smile that makes his eyes sparkle. He looks like a friendly grandpa or maybe the head of a mob family; I cannot quite decide. I motion to Chris that he is approaching us.

"Hello Tony," Chris says as he gives his friend a hug that looks a lot like a pat down.

I stand to greet my new friend with a little hesitation. How do I introduce myself to someone I have never met, when I need answers and am being chased by criminals with guns?

Chris turns to me and says, "Tony this is my friend Stella."

Tony replies, "Stella, *Ciao* Bella. Hello, welcome to our beautiful city. I hope you had a nice journey here. Are you hungry, pretty lady?" He rolls me into a large bear hug in the middle of the lobby like we are old friends.

I stand stock still with my arms at my sides. It feels odd to be hugged by a complete stranger, especially after the events of the last few days. Yet, as I step back, I smile. It's as if the hug made us family, and he had mentioned food. They are like magic words. I am starting to feel happier already.

I nod my head. "Yes," I say. "Food would be wonderful."

...and answers, I say to myself.

I let out a little laugh. It is approaching lunch time. The sound of my voice is odd to my ears. It is like I am trying too hard. Tony takes my hand and leads me from the lobby leaving Chris to follow behind us. Tony's hands are soft, and he smells of expensive cigars.

Tony continues to pepper me with questions about what kinds of food I like as we walk out of the lobby passing the hotel employee that had greeted us earlier. It feels nice to have a simple conversation. It seems so normal, like we are old friends catching up. I feel myself relaxing and enjoying the warm summer day. The warm sun feels good on my face. We head down the sidewalk around the corner to a café with outdoor seating.

The restaurant is busy, people seem happy to be here. The hostess leads us to a nice table for four next to the sidewalk but still under the awning, and she hands us all menus. We order a calamari appetizer for the table to start, and I get a seafood pasta dish for dinner. I ask for water, but Tony insists on ordering us a bottle of wine for the table to celebrate our visit and our new friendship. The speakers in the corner were playing a jazzy little piano number that, if I was feeling better, might have made me want to tap my feet. I am anxious for Tony's news. This entire day feels surreal like I am living someone else's life.

The wine arrives quickly, and the waitress pours us each a glass. "Thank you," I express to Tony as I raise my glass and take a sip. The men raise their glasses and we salute our new friendship. "Cheers," Chris says.

"Cheers," Tony adds.

"We need to know more about the intruders at Stella's home. Who were they working for?" Chris asks Tony.

I lean forward, waiting for Tony's answer. This could be the moment I learn what sparked John and Paul's abduction. The catalyst for it all. I hold my breath. Unfortunately, Tony does not answer the way I need.

"It is complicated. These guns that are being trafficked are worth a lot of money. I mean millions of dollars and that is not even including the military secrets that were sold. Whomever gets their hands on them is going to make a fortune it is what I hear on the street. These are state of the art primo pieces," Tony states nonchalantly like he is discussing the price of coffee at Starbucks.

"But do you know *who* wants them?" I ask cutting in.

"Ah, yes, everybody wants them, my dear lady. Everybody," Tony replies smiling at me. Tony's cell phone rings ending our questioning for the time being. I sit drinking my wine. Our food arrives and I take a few bites. I am impatient to ask Tony more questions about the guns. We had not even dived into the intruders or who could have taken John and Paul. I dig into my food realizing how hungry I am.

I feel warm and fuzzy. I think about millions of dollars.

We had extra money sure, but in no way did it all add up to millions of dollars.

Tony gets off the phone and orders another bottle of wine for the table. How did we finish the first bottle already? I look around. I am having a hard time focusing on the tourists as they walk by. The warm air feels nice. I hear the table next to us chatting about going to catch a movie. I feel like the music has been turned up a little and makes me want to dance. I look at Chris and think about how much I am starting to like him. I cannot stop laughing at Tony's jokes. I am not able to finish my pasta and am starting to feel light headed.

I start to think about something…something I am supposed to be working on, but I cannot catch my thoughts. They float away on the sunshine. I take a bite of the chocolate cake that is put in front me. My head is spinning. It cannot be from the wine. I only had a few glasses or did I…I cannot count back correctly. I am sure something is wrong, but I cannot put my finger on it. This meeting with Tony is not going down the path that I had hoped it would. I have no answers. Tony is a dead end.

Chapter 13

I am pretty sure I have a hangover. I cannot tell; my head hurts so much. I awake with no idea where I am. I know this sounds dumb, since I am not like that, but then I realize this is worse than waking up with hangover. I am lying on the floor. I open my eyes to see it is old wood, stained, with uneven planks and jagged pieces. The wood is patterned like water in a puddle forming circles and squiggles. There are darker stains in places and places where the color is light as if bleach was spilled. The floor is cool and doesn't really bother me much. I leave my head lying against it and shift my body slowly to see more of the room. There is a little bit of light coming in the window from a flashing yellow sign outside somewhere, or maybe a street lamp? It could even be the sun; I am having a hard time connecting the dots. The walls have peeling light green paint on them; they look as if layers of bad paint choices are dripping from the walls.

Ohhh, hell, my head hurts. The room spins. This is followed by the crushing feelings that I did not get the answers I needed to find Paul. I have no answers; I am sick and alone. I lay there and contemplate the paint colors on the wall. Light green; maybe gray. There could have been a white in there. I can barely open my eyes or lift my head off the floor. My stomach feels bad. The room spins. I close my eyes. I lay flat on my back, feeling the wood planks pressing against my head. The room smells like sweat, cigarettes, and stale beer. I feel too hot. I lay my hands flat on the floor to steady myself and open my eyes, looking at the chipped, water-stained ceiling. I cannot concentrate on any one thing. My body feels prickly. My mouth is dry. I hear men talking in low voices. Slowly, I make out the words. Guns, they are talking about making a trade for guns.

Trying to listen is too much. My head hurts. I have not felt this kind of pain all over my body before. I don't like the light coming into the room. I curl in a ball on my side trying to protect myself from it; sleep calls to me. I close my eyes, and I am comforted in the blackness.

I try to think but everything is too hard. I press my eyes closed against the pain.

What is wrong with me? Do I hear Tony's voice? Where is Chris?

I try to listen. Again, I hear voices, I hear someone talking about money, that they are going to make a lot of money when they have the guns. It is a small clue. My world goes black again and the room fades away.

Hours later, or it could be minutes later, I have no sense of time; I hear the door open from far away. A metal lock turns with a sharp click, and the hinges make a creaking sound as the old, gray door pushes open. I am trying to open my eyes, but my lids feel too heavy, they are stuck together. I feel sick and fuzzy. My stomach hurts, and my back aches. My hands are tingling as blood rushes into them. My body feels like it has been run over by a tank. Footsteps shuffle towards me. I squint to open my eyes. I am looking up at an angle with my head still resting on the wood floor. I realize I am still in the strange room with the peeling paint, lying on the floor.

A small, old woman with a scarf around her head is handing me a bowl. It has no smell and looks like cold, mushy noodles or potatoes. She smiles at me with one tooth sticking out of the bottom of her mouth. I take the bowl from her and she scurries away out the door. I watch her faded pink slippers retreat.

"Where?" I rasp out after her. Barely any sound escapes my cracked lips. I start to dry cough, and it hurts everywhere. I breathe in and get a whiff of things I do not want to think about. I breathe in again, a deep breath, and clean the sleep from my eyes. I am mad at myself for landing in this situation. I sit up and scoot backward, leaning against the wall with my bowl. I hear the lock click as someone pulls on the door to check that it is secure. The metal handle rattles as if it could fall off at any minute and roll across the floor.

My mind is spinning. I pick up a chunk of potato noodles with two fingers and put it in my mouth. I choke on it; my mouth is so dry. My body wants to reject the food. The potato noodles are cold, but I am hungry, I eat it. The food has no smell and almost no taste. I hope this food will settle my stomach. I need to feel better; I need my brain to focus on a plan to get out of here.

I have no idea how long I have been here. I look around. There is nothing in the room. I am still wearing my new outfit from the Mandarin hotel. I try to think back to the last thing I remember. I was having lunch with Chris and

Tony. We were eating dinner at an outdoor café and laughing. The pictures of the day slide through my mind. The glasses of wine and chocolate cake are the last things I remember. We were laughing. It is odd; I was laughing so much. Then nothing. My mind is blank. I do not know what happened after that or how I got to this room.

The door opens, and the small, old woman shuffles back in and hands me a plastic glass with water in it. She takes my bowl away.

As she turns to leave, I ask her, "Where am I?" in a whisper that I am not sure she hears or even understands.

She looks at me and smiles, closing the door. Her faded pink slippers move the dust out of the room in front of her. I finish my water and lay the glass down carefully. I curl back into a ball on the floor. My head is still pounding. I am working hard not to throw-up as there is no bowl or place for my stomach contents to go except here on the floor with me. I put my hands under my head and try to rest. I close my eyes again pushing away the pain. Behind my lids, John is there, waiting for me. He is dancing around our old house, holding baby Paul. I stand in our kitchen and watch. We start to laugh. When I wake again, it is night, and the flashing light is coming in through the window.

I sit up and move against the wall, a little unsteady on my feet. The wall feels rough against my skin. The room has not been painted in many years. The wall color might have once been a pale blue underneath the peeling white. The wooden window frames have seen better days. I realize that I have been drugged and kidnapped. No one is looking for me, and I am alone somewhere in the world. It is hard to imagine what happened to me, how I got here, or even where here is. Or what day of the week it is. I feel battered and bruised. Every part of me hurts. My stomach is still queasy.

I inch towards the window and carefully use my hand to lift the thin, yellowed sheet that is covering the opening. I look out into the dark night through the metal window security bars. I quickly realize I am still in D.C. I can see the tip of the Washington Monument across the buildings.

"I am still in Washington D.C.," I say aloud, as if it is a prayer.

Knowing where I am is somewhat comforting. I close my eyes and sink down against the wall, wrapping my arms around my knees. Moving has taken a lot out of me and my stomach is rebelling again. I start to dry heave as I hold on to the wall. The motion hurts my ribs. My head starts to spin.

"At least I know where I am," I say quietly to the empty room.

My body is wiped out. I crawl back down to the floor. I think back to the days before all of this craziness started. My life, our life, my handsome husband, my son, my home in Fayetteville, North Carolina.

Pictures start to flash through my mind of days gone by. A few years ago, John and me, sipping champagne on our new back porch, enjoying the moonlight while he points out the constellations overhead. These images are all that is left of our life. Those happy times do not feel like that long ago. But they could belong to someone else now. I hold my stomach wishing it would stop its war against my body. I do not want to throw-up in here.

Tears start to run down my face, and I rock myself back and forth against the wall. My eyes start to burn. I use my blue shirt to wipe my face and chin. My tears are silent, too painful to express out loud, too hard to explain even to myself. I slide further down the wall and sit on the floor across from the window looking up at the metal bars that block my exit. I unbuckle the wedge sandals I am still wearing and rub my ankles.

"Stella, what are you going to do now?" I ask out loud.

I push my shoes to the side. They were a dumb idea. I did not need new wedge sandals to find my son. I lick my tears off my lips and pull my hands through my hair. The old lady with the head scarf shuffles in and hands me another small bowl of cold noodles to eat. I did not hear the door unlock or swing open, I was too caught up in berating myself.

"Bathroom?" I ask softly. "Please?" I beg her with my eyes.

She turns and walks quietly to the door. She raises her hand, motioning at me to come.

All I had to do was ask?

I am incredulous.

Maybe, I can just ask to leave then?

I laugh to myself like all of this is some kind of twisted joke or escape room game at the mall. I stand up, a little shakily, and tentatively walk to the door in my bare feet, leaving the stupid wedge sandals behind. My steps make the old, wooden floor boards creak. Outside my door, a man wearing dark slacks and a white undershirt sits at a small laminate kitchen table, watching a soccer game on TV. He is smoking—chain smoking it looks like by the full ashtray sitting next to him. It smells terrible. I try to hold my breath as my stomach rebels. The room is small and sparsely filled with furniture. It looks like Archie Bunker

93

decorated it. The old lady points to a door in front of me with a thin, crooked, cigarette-stained finger. Her yellowed nail highlights the way.

I walk into an old bathroom that looks like it has been around since the 1950s and needs a good cleaning. In another life, I would have walked out and held it. Today, I do not care. It is rusty and falling apart. The water tank above the seat has a pull string. The whole thing looks like it is going to break apart if I touch it. There is a strong moldy and damp odor. The old, metal sink is chipped and pitted, and the faucet drips a stream of water down a rust stain on the graying basin. The tight space is wallpapered with large, bright-pink flowers that have faded and are coming up at the seams. All of the fixtures are covered with pink carpet. The mirror is almost unusable and barely hanging on above the sink. I am afraid to look at myself as I step toward the mirror, closing the door behind me. There is no lock.

I finish my business quickly, moving to wash my face and hands. I shakily splash water down my front and into my hair. I take a deep breath and choke on the smell. I stop for a moment and look straight into the cracked mirror. My face looks dull and sunken in the mirror. I do not recognize myself. I carefully touch my cheek. My hair badly needs to be brushed. I wet it with more water from the sink and run my hands through it slowly. As if straightening my hair would help make my world a better place, I continue to groom myself in the mirror.

Suddenly, a loud knock on the door startles me out of my thoughts. The old lady opens the bathroom door and raises her bony hand to me. I splash water on to my hands and arms once more. It is time to go back to my room. As I carefully step around the edge of the room near the wall in my bare feet, I see cigarette guy holding a gun. He smiles at me, pointing the gun and making a shooting motion like it is a toy. His toothy leer makes my stomach tighten. I need a plan to get out of here and save myself.

The smell of the cigarettes is overpowering, and my stomach turns again. I hurry to my door and into the corner of my room, as far away from him as possible, where I had left my bowl of cold potato noodles on the floor. The old lady brings me another glass of water. I thank her as she shuffles away in her pink slippers. It is better to have a friend than an enemy. She does not look at me but simply closes and locks the door behind her.

I sit on the hard, bare floor and eat my sad, little bowl of food, sighing to myself. Before I know it, I have fallen asleep again with my head resting against the wall in the corner. John is there. We are walking on the beach in Anguilla. Bright sunsets and clear blue water surround us. It seems the old lady is spiking my cold potato noodles.

Suddenly, Chris is yelling at me in my dream, "Wake-up!"

I awake to someone rubbing my arm. I am overwhelmed by the smell of cigarettes and stale beer. My body is curled against the wall. I cannot quite open my eyes, but I feel a sense of dread. A strange hand cups my breast. I want to shout; but I cannot make a sound. A hand moves over my mouth, hot breath is on my neck. The smell of the cigarettes permeates everything around me. My heart is hammering in my chest. My eyes finally open in the dark, and the light flashing outside my window makes it hard to focus. The cigarette man is holding me against the wall. I try to move a few inches away from him, but it is no use. I am trapped between him and the wall. He pushes my face into the corner.

I can barely make out the form of the old lady when she quietly shuffles in, carrying the gun in a shadow. She aims it at the man and starts fusses at him in Italian. I get the impression that he is her son. She is upset, gesturing at him to move away from me, and he yells back at her to get out waving his arm in the air. His motion gives me space to move my body, but it is no use, I still cannot raise my arms or move my body away from his attack. I am pinned in. He kicks the bottle of beer he has laid next to him. The contents spill out onto the floor wetting my capris as the bottle rolls towards me. It sounds like a bicycle chain ticking through its gears. The stink of cheap beer surrounds me. I shrink against the wall, trying to press myself back into the plaster, trying to disappear. I must escape. I cannot stay here.

The old lady reaches in and pushes him away from me. She is stronger than I imagined. They continue to argue, pointing at each other. I watch them as I pull my clothes tight around me. They move out of the room. I realize that I need to go.

Now.

Suddenly, I am annoyed at myself for sitting here. I make a decision.

I stand up and move over to the window. I cannot go through the bars on the window. Even if I could climb down from this window, it is too high. I review my options.

Their angry voices carry away from me as they move through the apartment. I look back over my shoulder at the door; it is sitting open. I walk slowly over to it, trying not to make a sound and peer out, hiding behind the door like a small child. No one is around. I can still hear shouting. They mention that Tony wants the guns and money, but I cannot see them from this angle. The man is yelling that I know where the guns are, the woman that they need the money. I understand now that I was to lead them to the guns or maybe be exchanged for the guns that they were going to sell for money. The old woman is yelling about me, that he should not be touching me. Tony wants the guns. I hear the man talk about the colonel. Someone slams something into a table or hits a wall. There is a loud clap.

I cautiously step from my room and sneak past the smoker's ashtray-filled table toward the kitchen. There is a cigarette still burning in the ashtray. I scan the room with wild eyes. Startled, I see another man, who is asleep; he snores loudly on the couch. The noise panics me like a small animal caught in the headlights of an incoming car. I grab my chest and stand very still. I had not noticed him before.

I listen hard; the old lady and the smoker continue to argue. I hear the words "guns" and "money" again, like the intruders in my home my kidnapping has been about the guns. I do not know anything about the missing guns. I do know this is my chance to escape from these crazy people. I cannot wait on Chris to appear this time and save me.

I must save myself. I can save myself. I will not be used as a pawn for guns.

My heart is beating loudly in my ears. The front door out to the apartment is right in front of me. I run for the door like an Olympic sprinter taking long strides. I reach out, it's locked or stuck. I grab and pull at the old-fashioned handle with both hands and turn, jerking the door open. I dash into the hallway and look to my right and left like a caged animal. I am sure they are going to haul me back in, to shoot me. I look over the railing and see the way out.

I am about four floors up in an old brown stone. I dash down the stairs. There is no air in the musty and oppressive hallway. The stairs are timeworn and slippery. There is almost no light, and dark shadows are shrouded in the corners. I do not have time to be frightened. I run like the devil is hunting me. Plummeting down the steps, grasping for the rails, stumbling into the walls. I have not used my legs in a bit and stumble like a new born colt; they have a tough time remembering how to go fast. I trip and stagger like a drunk. I gasp for breath and my feet slap against the wood. I keep going.

I lurch for the railing, zigzagging my way to the floors below. I am breathing hard. Trash litters the landings. Spray paint covers the walls. I gulp in the stench and push myself to continue, holding my side. I want to throw-up. My stomach is a mixture of fear, heavy-duty drugs, and disgusting food. I must get away.

I make it to the bottom and shove open the substantial wooden entrance door, using all of my body weight to push against it. I beat it with my fists. Finally, it releases from its position and throws me out onto the stairs and down to the sidewalk. My feet are jumbled beneath me, and I fall onto my back side in the street. The first thing I notice is that it is a warm, nice night, and people are out and about. The second thing is that the concrete I have fallen onto is pitied, and I have scrapped my hands. They tingle painfully. I quickly stand up and fall straight into a good-looking young couple holding hands. They are dressed for a date and back away from me with a fearful look on their faces.

Their fear of me registers, and I realize they probably think I am a crazed drug addict trying to steal their money. I look up at the sky and take a deep breath of the clean air steadying myself.

I have freed myself. I need to run and get away from this place.

I smooth my hair with my scrapped hands and try to find my way. I turn in a circle, feeling the harsh pavement that scrapped my hands under my bare feet. The concrete is mixed with sharp stones. My breathing slows, but my heart is still going too fast in my ears. I have escaped the apartment. I am free of my captors. They can no longer use me to get the guns.

I want to cheer. My mind cannot focus.

Cars are driving by. An older man is out for a walk across the street with his dog. The noise and lights are loud but familiar. I must still have a lot of drugs in my system. Life is moving about like a circus. I hear music and people laughing. Down the street, the cafés are full of people eating and drinking. I breathe again and smell food. It turns my stomach and I heave, almost falling to the ground.

I feel like a baby alone in the world for the first time. Everything pushes into me with an intensity that is frightening and awakening. I am smiling like a loon, but I cannot stop. My adrenaline rush has left me euphoric kicking the leftover drugs into hyper drive. I want to shout about my kidnappers and jump up and down like a child trying to get attention. My head is a mess of ideas, moving sounds and colors assault me from every direction.

I walk down the middle of the sidewalk, turning this way and that. I falter like a drunken sailor and constantly peek behind me to see if I have been followed. But no one is there. People move out of my way. I recognize the scent of pizza baking. I hold my clothes tight around me.

I look down.

I fixate on the fact that I have no shoes on my feet. I notice my feet are dirty. The sidewalk is rough, and it hurts. I start to inspect my hands they have pieces of ground stuck in them. I am getting drowsy. It is hard to focus on what I need to do. I push forward. I have no idea how many hours or days have passed since I was kidnapped. I do not know where I am.

I march forward until I spot a church on the corner. I pause on the sidewalk and look up. "Would they find me here?" I ask out loud. No one answers me. I look around.

I do not even know who "they" are except that they work for Tony and want guns and or money for me. I slowly open one of the large carved doors; it is almost too heavy for me. The weight is staggering, and I pull hard. I tentatively slide inside, one dirty, bare foot at a time. The door scrapes the floor and makes a shushing sound. The sanctuary is empty. The air conditioner is on, and the cool air hits me in the face, surrounding me. I smell candles.

As the door floats closed, I notice how quiet it is as compared to the outside. All the noise has stopped. The tiled floor is cold on my feet. The church is beautiful, all stained glass and holiness. I feel bizarre standing there, dirty with my feet bare and drugged. I reach up to smooth my hair down, and I touch the heart and key necklace Paul had given me, comforted that I still have it.

I drift a few feet inside; tentatively, like a frightened dog that has been kicked too many times. I am waiting for someone to shout at me for being here. I let my hands touch the wood of the pews. I glide into one softly. The polished wood is gleaming. Someone takes good care of this place. I glide my hand over the wood, appreciating its sturdiness. I try not to make any noise as I sit there, staring at the altar and at Jesus on the cross. I feel like a child. I am tired, so very tired. My eye lids start to flutter down. The adrenaline from my escape is gone. The days of very little food and water are catching up with me. The drugged potato noodles are still in my system. Slowly, I sink to my knees onto the timeworn wooden bench and start to soundlessly pray. I am compelled. My hands clasp together in front of me like a child praying before bed.

I mumble the words to myself in a whisper, "Hail Mary, full of grace, the Lord is with thee. Blessed art thou among women, and blessed is the fruit of thy womb, Jesus. Holy Mary, Mother of God, pray for us sinners, now and at the hour of our death. Amen."

I do not know where the words come from, maybe some old forgotten childhood memory of church with my parents, but they calm my heart. I kneel on the bench, gazing forward, hands together, praying for a miracle to save me from this nightmare that is my life. Tears start to fall from my eyes. I pray because I know my strength is leaving me. I pray for John, hoping he is able to protect Paul. John may have done things that have wrecked our marriage and horrible things with guns, but I trust him to take care of our son. I pray for Paul, who deserves so much better than all of this. I vow to find Paul no matter what it takes. I sit there and thoughts of my son comfort me.

I wonder what happened to Chris. *Was he involved in my kidnapping or did something bad happen to him too?* I thank whatever spirit sent him to me in my dream to save me from the smoker who wanted to touch me. A shudder racks my body at the thought of the smoker's hands on me. I continue to sit in silence, praying for a way out of this chaos. The peace of the church envelopes me. The smell of old, polished wood calms me.

I am dirty, homeless, high, alone, and no closer to finding Paul. Meeting with Tony had been a mistake, Chris's mistake, but I went along with it. I am desperate for answers. The strength I tapped to escape my captors has left me. The drugs from the kidnapping flow through my system. I may have escaped the apartment where they were holding me, waiting to exchange me for guns, or hoping I would take them to the guns, but I am no closer to finding Paul. I hold on to my necklace tightly trying to connect with Paul. I am safe for the moment. I have saved myself; that is something to proud of today. Tomorrow, I will do more.

Chapter 14

I come alert to someone touching me; a wispy memory of the smoker surfaces and frightens me. This time, though, the person is not grabbing me, but tapping me lightly on the shoulder and speaking softly in Spanish. The words sound comforting. The voice is soft and warm. I am confused. I pull myself up and turn to face my attacker, raising my hand and getting ready to run. In that moment, I realize I have fallen asleep praying for help in the beautiful little church. My knees ache. I am getting too old for this. I have been holding my head up with my hand like a teenager trying not to fall asleep in math class. The man tapping me on the shoulder wears the telltale black suit and white collar of a priest. His warm eyes look at me expectantly. I have no idea what he is saying. I spoke some Spanish when I was working at the University of Miami but had not used it in years, except maybe to order drinks on vacation in Mexico. *Cerveza* and *gracias* are not going to help me now.

The words the priest is saying sound familiar, but I have no idea what they are. My wits were not at their sharpest after everything I have been through.

I whisper, "English?"

The young priest chuckles a little and smiles. "Oh, I am so glad you can hear me. I thought you might be deaf, and I do not know sign language. Can I help you? We cannot let people sleep in the sanctuary. I apologize, but we do not take in the homeless here. I can direct you to a homeless shelter or call the police if you are in trouble. I apologize for the Spanish. We had a lot of immigrants looking for shelter lately and I am doing my best to help them find their way."

His appearance, the clean black suit and white starched collar, look so normal in the church. I am comforted by his presences even though he is young and asking me to leave. A strange thought about the movie *Thorn Birds* flits through my mind. He is pretty good looking to have given his life to the church. The thought makes me smile a little. I sit back on the wooden bench looking down at my dirty, drugged-out, barefoot appearance and stare at him, unsure of what to say, embarrassed. *Where do I start? How much should I tell this man of the cloth?* I smooth my hair down and try to find the words to explain how I came here. I can do this. For Paul, I must be strong.

"I am an American. I do not speak Spanish or need a homeless shelter. My name is Stella," I speak to him slowly, trying out the words. "I need the police."

He smiles at me like I am a child and offers me his hand helping me to rise form the bench.

The police officers came to the church and took down my story. I was sorry to leave the church; it was the first place I had felt safe in days. We made a stop at the hospital for a check because of the drugs in my system. The questions I was asked made me glad I had escaped from the smoker when I did. It was embarrassing and comforting to have the nurses care about what had happened to me. It made me realize there are good people left in the world. Once I finished there, an officer escorted me to the station for questioning. They wanted to find where I had been held and help me reconstruct a drawing of my kidnappers. All the details are pretty fuzzy. I have been in the police station for hours. The room is painted cream and has big wooden desks lined up like soldiers standing at attention. The floor is tiled in mosaics, like the room had once been used for something better than a police station. My eyes have been following the patterns of pretty colors on the floor. The ceiling has lovely crown molding on it as well. I keep busy, cataloging all the nice features, trying not to fall asleep. The drugs from the old lady are slow to leave me system. The doorframes in the room are extra-large. The walls have maps of the city on them and signs of past city parades and marathons hanging on them. Some of the desks have lots of papers stacked on them, and a few have pictures in frames of smiling families. It is quiet in the station today. Not much seems to happen here on Sundays.

A small, white fan is blowing on the desk in the front of me, oscillating back and forth. All of the people here are so nice to me. I tell them my name and that I do not know what happened to me. I tell them I awoke in a room and was kept in an apartment. I say I do not know a lot.

How did I get there? I do not know. Who are these people? I do not know.

Why would they want you? It has to do with guns, I think.

What guns? I am not sure yet, but I think they are my husband's.

Where were you taken from? A café near the Hay Adams hotel I was having dinner with a man who was going to help me.

Why would he help you? I do not know. Who were you traveling with? Chris!

Chris who? I do not know. I think he works for the CIA What were you doing in D.C? We were having dinner with Tony. Who is Tony? I do not know.

And around and round the questions go. I have a headache.

How long were you in the room? I do not know, maybe two days.

It was Thursday when we went to dinner. It was Monday when my husband's Jeep exploded in my driveway. It was Wednesday when intruders broke into my home and burned it down.

I start to tick off the facts I know.

It was Tuesday when I found the note in my husband's pocket from Rain.

I keep that to myself.

The police man smiles at me a lot. I have the feeling he thinks I am a delusional woman that has lost her way. My story does not make sense even to me. They keep asking me for my identification. I do not have any. Everything I had is in Fayetteville.

I want answers. They want answers.

I have no purse or ID, no money, not even any shoes.

I do not have any answers. I want to scream at someone.

I stare down at my dirty bare feet. I had cleaned up a little in the washroom, but I know I still look a wreck. The police do not have any more answers for me than I have for them. The small television stuck in the corner of the room has the news on. A pretty, blonde newscaster is reporting that a new *Star Wars* is breaking records at the box office. I look down at my grimy clothes. I am starting to feel sorry for myself. It is time to tell someone my whole story. As a new police officer sets a fresh cup of coffee next to me with a smile, I grab his arm. I lay it out for him no more, "I don't know." As much as I can, I tell my story.

"Let's stop with the questions; they are getting us nowhere. Let me tell you what I do know."

I start with John, our Memorial Day pool party, the bomb in my front yard—"the event"—losing John and Paul. I describe my day of questions with Agent Scott of the FBI. I talk about the storm and the men demanding guns that burned down my home, Agent Chris of the CIA saving me from the intruders at my house, Lori at the Mandarin hotel giving me a room to clean-up, meeting Tony for dinner hoping for answers or a lead to find my son, waking up in the room with the cold spiked noodles, and escaping from the old lady and the man with the gun who tried to touch me. It all comes pouring out, everything that has happened to me in this week since Monday and our pool party. My story sounds so unreal. It is cathartic to unravel my story, as if a dam has broken inside me. I replay the scenes for the police officer as if I am telling him about a James Bond movie instead of my life. I stand up and walk back and forth pacing before him, moving my hands around to paint the pictures as I talk. At the end, when I have no more to say, the young police officer looks at me and replies in his strong Boston accent.

"That is a wicked tale. Let me call the FBI, maybe this Agent Scott in Fayetteville can help you."

I can tell he does not believe me, but I do not care at this point. He picks up the phone on his desk and starts to make some phone calls. I sit back and sip my coffee. It has grown cold and bitter. I make a face. Hopefully, someone will believe me. I still need to find Paul. It has been almost a week since he was taken with his father.

Within an hour, a smart looking man in white button down with a navy-blue sport coat and jeans from the local FBI office arrives to fetch me. It all happens very briskly. The police officer hands me over to him with some paperwork. They sign forms and show badges. It is all very official, like I am a FedEx package changing hands. The police officer smiles at me, and I can tell he is glad to get back to his life without me there. He is used to peaceful days at the office, not kidnapped victims high on gnocchi drugs telling incredible stories of criminal intrigue. Gnocchi, I learned from the officer, was what the old lady had been feeding me. It was the one thing he could explain to me about what happened.

The smart-looking FBI man, Phillip, hands me a pair of black sweatpants, a gray T-shirt, white flip-flops, and a small bag of toiletry items. It seems to be a sort of FBI refugee package. I change into my newly issued clothes in the ladies' room, washing up in the sink. This bathroom is better than the old, pink one in the apartment but not by much. I hesitate a moment before I throw the capris and the blue top in the trash. They stink and are disgusting, but they are mine. I own so little these days, but they remind me of the smoker.

I let them slip through my hands and into the silver metal trash can, hitting the bottom before I can change my mind. Before I leave the police station with Phillip, I thank the police officer for his help. No need to burn bridges, I may be back here someday with the way my life is going full speed into crazy town. I need more friends and less enemies. I quickly shake his hand and walk out to the FBI man's car. The night is overcast, and the moon is hiding behind the clouds; it is still warm out. Phillip's car is a black, two-door Prius with an automatic transmission.

The dark interior is spotless; it makes me think again about my current un-showered appearance. I sit in the passenger seat and put my seat belt on. Phillip does not talk to me or even look at me as he gets in the automobile and drives us away from the police station. The radio comes on playing a local news station. I gaze out the window and observe the passing streets of the city as we move towards the National Mall Monuments into the more touristy side of town. Here I am, again, driving with another man I do not even know. I am past heeding the stranger danger scenario that has popped into my mind. I need a shower, real food, and some answers. I lean back in the seat and try to think of a plan to save my son. The more I go through what has happened, what I have survived this week, the more I am sure that I can do this. It is now Saturday night; it has been 6 full days since Paul and John went missing and all I know for sure is that they were on private plane that left the country. I saved myself from the apartment having been kidnapped for guns, and I can save Paul, too. A new inner strength hits me. I will find a way to protect my son and find our way back home.

Chapter 15

Sunday comes to me as a day to rest and rebuild myself, the tree-lined street is crowded with tourists posing for pictures, laughing and talking about their day of site seeing. The air hangs warm and heavy in the city. I have had a full day of trying to put myself back together and now the sun is setting beyond the buildings, sending a warm glow through the streets and narrow alleys. I sit alone at a table for two near Dupont circle, sipping a fruity non-alcoholic spritzer from the restaurant's menu; it came in a pretty goblet with a slice of orange. The tiled table has an attractive, colorful mosaic pattern. I follow the pattern with my finger. I breathe in the warm air and try to clear my mind. The panic that spirals inside me is always near the surface. Frank Sinatra drifts to me from somewhere close by singing *All the way*. The song makes me smile, a sad smile. I feel lost and alone. I am losing hope that I will find Paul and John. It has been 7 days; I lost them, and our home. The sadness hits me like a freight train. It is a lot to bare on my own.

I know I cannot stay out here long as darkness descends on the city. I will feel safer in my room with the door securely locked. Between the intruders in my home and being kidnapped, I have developed certain fears, certain instincts of self-preservation with all that has happened over the last 7 days. I remind myself that I am okay, it has been less than 24 hours since the room with the old lady with pink slippers and a head scarf, the cold potato Gnocchi, my harrowing escape, and the beautiful little church. The police have located the apartment where I was kept, and it is now empty there is no sign of my kidnappers. They seem to have disappeared into the vapor like John and Paul.

I am staying in the Kimpton hotel down the street from this little restaurant awaiting my new identification. I can go home to Fayetteville tomorrow, Monday. Phillip and I had talked for hours until the sun came up, and he finally took me to a hotel to get some rest. He wanted me to repeat the story I had told the police officer. Phillip wanted the details on my kidnapping and why I thought they were holding me for guns. I also had to give a detailed description on Tony.

Phillip and I are not what you might call friends, but he has become friendly. I know my story is incredible, and I'm trying to give Phillip the benefit of the doubt. He is a nice man with a wife and two daughters who is only trying to do his job. He did not talk much to me about his life. It is like I have a disease that he might catch. My crazy might infect him.

I have access to my bank accounts down in North Carolina, and my hotel room is nice. I was able to buy some clean, new clothes this afternoon, which made me feel confident enough to leave my hotel room. It is the little things like this that I am feeling grateful for as I move forward. I probably would not be eating cold noodles or drinking red wine with strangers again for a very long time. I sip my drink and think about what I had learned from Phillip.

My home had burned down, John is officially listed as a criminal by the army, and both John and Paul were still missing. Phillip at the FBI could not find a Chris at the CIA, but I did not know his last name or even if Chris was his real first name. It could have been his middle name or an alias. I let my hand smack the table at my ignorance, causing my drink glass to shutter. The romantic couple at the next table regard me over their clasped hands.

I had assisted with a composite drawing of Chris and Tony for the FBI. Fortunately, Tony did show up in the database. Tony is a real mobster, and me, a regular person from Fayetteville, North Carolina, should never have encountered him. Tony is into drugs, human trafficking, and guns. I try not to reflect on my time in the apartment too much. Overall, this week has brought more questions than answers.

My life is going full-speed ahead in a Jason Bourne movie fashion. I look at my short-trimmed nails tapping against my almost-empty glass and wonder if I will ever feel normal again. I gaze down at my new, pink flats under the table. They are pretty, but I really do not care about shoes anymore. I required more than the FBI refugee package to keep some clothes on my body.

As I lower my glass to the tiled table, I spot a woman who looks like she is watching me from across the street. I squint, focusing on her. She is a tall, thin blonde, and she is looking straight at me. It is strange, I know her; I am applying all my brainpower, struggling to place the woman as she strolls in my direction. The blonde woman has on a slick, navy-blue pantsuit with a white blouse underneath. Her shoes appear to be black half boots with a zipper on the side. Her outfit is clean and crisp, no extra jewelry or colors are visible, not even a girly purse. She carries a shopping bag that looks large and out of place with her uniform-like outfit.

All at once, it comes to me. This is Jane, Colonel Steve's new wife, except she does not look like the lady who had attended our Memorial Day house party in the red polka dot dress. My mind flashes to Jane and Steve sitting in my backyard; to Jane holding me back from the fire; to Jane standing next to me as the investigation team asks questions; to Jane calling to check on me. Suddenly, it occurs to me that Jane had rather strongly held me back from the fire. How had she reacted so fast? Why had Jane, the new, young, pretty wife who had come to our pool party over-dressed, rushed to the front of the house with the soldiers instead of helping with the children and staying in the safety of the backyard?

The scene of the Jeep on fire and the flames falling into my front yard, as I was being held back, flashes before my eyes. It is a picture straight out of a war movie. I move my hand to my eyes to wipe it away. I do not want to go there right now. I will become too emotional sitting in the restaurant. All of my tears and worries are just beneath the surface.

The new, serious version of Jane walks up to my table and gracefully slides into the empty chair across from me.

"Hi, Stella," she clips out without any trace of a Texas accent. Even her smile seems different, more confident somehow. Her make-up is conservative today and pretty without adding a lot of color to her face; it is so different from how I knew her in Fayetteville. I stare across the table. She reaches into the shopping bag, grabs a purse from the bottom of the bag, and lays it on the table between us. The waiter walks up.

"Good evening, may I get you something to drink?"

"No, thank you," Jane replies as she waives him away.

I stare at my old purse on the table. It is the Coach purse that I left in my Volvo in the driveway in Fayetteville that stormy night when I had fled with Chris. It seems a lifetime ago. I reach out and touch the soft material between my fingers. It is real. I do not say anything. I reach inside with Jane watching me and find my iPhone. I hold it up and press the on button. It is dead. I stare at it like I had never seen one before. I do not know what to say.

Finally, Jane speaks carefully and quietly like she is trying not to frighten me away.

"Stella, I have been searching for you. It took me some time to find you after you went missing from your home in Fayetteville. The fire burned any evidence, and I could not track you on cameras. There are just not enough of them. I thought I had caught up to you in DC; a camera caught you on street the other night not far from the Mandarin Oriental, but you were gone without a trace before I could find your trail. I brought your purse from your car so you would know I am a someone you can trust even if I am not who you thought I was. I am here to help you," Jane speaks gently and compassionately, like an old friend talking someone off a ledge.

"Here to help me?" I respond, confused and angry. Where was she when my husband and son were taken, when my home was burned to the ground, or when I was kidnapped, drugged, and groped? My thoughts are a jumble. I run my hands along the trim of the purse. That is when I could have used some help, not sitting here in alone at this nice restaurant.

"Yes," Jane states. "I need to tell you I am not who you think I am, and I want you to trust me because I can help you."

My mind registers that she is speaking to me as if I had been in an accident, slowly and watchfully. I twirl the straw in my drink glass and look out across the restaurant at the other diners. A few moments ago, this place seemed so idyllic and calming. I think about her offer; I am tired of trusting everyone and being left with nothing.

"Okay, Jane, who are you?" I reply in a tired, cold voice.

I turn and look her straight in the eyes, laying my glass down on the table and leaning in. I am angry. All the lies and the people who are trying to help me but seem to have their own agenda. A new, powerful feeling bubble up inside of me, one that is red hot and angry, replacing the old, sad and tired melancholy that was a part of me a few minutes ago. Inside a force is moving, eating up all the sad and replacing it with a new determination to not be the victim, to not just go along, to be the one in charge. I stare straight at Jane, waiting for her to divulge to me how she fits into my story. I am not going to be taken in so easily this time, not like with Chris. There are no intruders with guns pointed at us.

Jane glances at our surroundings and stands up, reaching for my hand.

"Let's go for a walk. The things I have to say are not for civilian ears." She lays twenty dollars on the table. I look it at and then her hand. I do not know if

I want to go with her, this new Jane, but I do know I want to hear what she has to say.

"Let's get on with it," I say as if I am facing a firing squad. I stand to join her, grabbing my things, including my old Coach purse.

She starts speaking slowly, watching around us as we walk back towards my hotel, "My name is Jane Phoenix. I work on a special team inside the CIA that tracks people selling weapons that originate in the United States to people overseas. We were created after 9/11 to utilize special technology to help fight terrorism in the world through a joint effort among many different countries." I put up my hand to stop her.

"What were you doing in my backyard pretending to be married to Colonel Steve then?" I am not sure if I want the answer.

"I was tracking a gun runner," Jane replies matter-of-factly, as if people talk of guns every day.

"Who did you think was involved in this plot at my home?" I snap at her, grabbing her arm and wrenching her around to face me. Jane calmly takes my hand and leads me to the side of the street against a course, dark red brick wall, looking to see if anyone had noticed our exchange. A shiny, silver BMW is parked on the sidewalk, blocking us from people in a nearby restaurant.

"*Jane,*" I cry out, again, not wanting her answer. I know the answer, but I need her to say it. She grips my wrist. My stomach is in a panic. My heart beats wildly. I need the words stated out loud. I grip Jane's arm harder with my free hand. She looks at my hand on her arm. Straightening her shoulders, she looks into my eyes and says the name I had feared, the name I knew she would say.

"John," she whispers.

The name echoes through my heart. Instantly, my hand moves from her arm to slap her. She knew and had done nothing to save me from all of this. Jane blocks it easily and pushes me up against the wall in one fluid movement. Jane's training is evident. She whispers in my ear like a lover. I can feel the heat from her breath.

"Stop, Stella. Listen to me. I am not here to hurt you. I think we can help each other."

We stand against the warm, hard brick wall as if locked in an embrace. Jane has me pinned. She is stronger than she looks. My breathing slows to normal. I look into her eyes. I do not want to hear what she has to say next, but then again, I do, don't I? I need these answers, these cold hard facts. My life has gone from normal to strange and to worse. I already know about John and Rain. I am lost in my whirling thoughts when, abruptly, Jane's voice breaks through my inner turmoil.

"Stella, we need to move. I think we are being followed."

She grabs my hand and holds it, leading me away from the wall toward my hotel. Jane is moving fast. She looks calm. This is Jane the actress, the chameleon, the spy, doing her job. I look nervously around. What did Jane see that I did not? In that moment, I want to be Jane. I want to be trained to see, to act, to be more than I am. I want to find the people that took my son, my life, and tried to kill me. I want to fight and be someone that they would be afraid to mess with because after everything I had been through lately, I have nothing left to lose.

I stumble a little in my new flats as I follow Jane. So much for being a bad-ass. I shake my head. One week of crazy in my life does not make me a CIA agent. Jane holds me up and continues walking, not looking back. She reaches inside her jacket. *She has a gun.* Of course, she has a gun, she is a CIA agent. She is some sort of super spy, and I am a wife and mom from Fayetteville. I almost laugh out loud as we hurry down the sidewalk and into the front lobby of my hotel.

The lobby is crowded with tourists getting ready to go out to dinner. Families were standing around the lobby meeting up and waiting. Jane goes straight through, not stopping to look for anything. A lady in an amazing cobalt blue dress and super high heels steps off the elevator as Jane pulls me inside. The lady smiles at us like we are a couple.

Quietly she asks, "Do you have your room key?" I nod my head *yes.*

I reach into my new wallet to pull it out.

I do not have much to say. I am dog-tired of being handled, of being out of the loop, of being a part of this—whatever this is! I tap the key against my palm, feeling a little anxious about this new turn of events. It is like I was given only a few hours of calm before being thrown back into the crazy today. This is a deadly and bizarre world that John and the CIA brought to my door.

Jane steps off the elevator, holding me back with her hand so she can inspect the hallway. Jane seems to know exactly what she is doing. Slowly, she escorts me out of the elevator, down the corridor, and to my door. Jane takes the key from my hand and opens the door. We step in, and I sit on the bed like a child. She bolts the door, thoroughly checks the bathroom, and pulls the blinds down on the windows. Finally, she sits across from me, pulling over the only chair in the room from the desk. Jane takes a deep breath, puts her hands on her lap, and prepares to tell me the story of how she ended up at my house on Memorial Day.

I inspect her appearance, this new Jane. She is fit, athletic looking, probably a little older than I had thought when I was made to believe she was married to Steve. Her nails are short and unpolished, her makeup is almost nonexistent, maybe a little mascara. It is hard to believe this is the same Jane I knew in Fayetteville. I shake my head and think to myself; I do not know this Jane or whoever this woman is. She does not even smell like that Jane. At our pool party, she smelled of expensive spring time flowers; now, she seems sterile in her uniform.

"Okay, Jane let's start in Fayetteville. How did you end up in my back yard on Memorial Day?"

Jane takes another deep breath, looks at her watch, and replies quietly as if deciding how much or what to tell me.

"I was looking for a traitor, a double agent, selling secrets about troop deployments, top secret missions, and weapons cachets. I followed a trail that led me to Ft. Bragg, then to John's Special Forces unit, and then to John. Steve agreed to help us by letting me pretend to be his wife. We had to get close. We had to be sure." It all came back to John.

"Jane, does Chris really work with you at the CIA? What happened to Chris when I was kidnapped? I hate to say this, but I think he might have been in on it…I don't know, I wanted to trust him, but then we met with his friend and then I was kidnapped. I don't know who to believe anymore."

"Yes, Chris is a CIA agent. He was beaten up pretty badly and dumped in a nearby parking garage by Tony's men. It looks like he was also drugged during your meeting with Tony. That is how they got the jump on him. He should have never gone in without backup. Since his wife died, he has been dealing with some issues around the CIA. My working theory is, maybe, he was trying to protect you from us."

I feel reassured that Chris did not leave me. Chris and I were trying to get answers and dinner with Tony backfired, putting us both in more danger. Chris may have made a mistake, but he was trying to do the right thing for me. He was trying to help me.

John is the one who hurt me. I cannot believe I did not see what was going on. I sit there and think about all the expensive things I had been buying to remodel our home in Fayetteville. John had not said a word about my spending. I had not paid attention, maybe I had not wanted to, until it was too late. If I had confronted John more about his time away, maybe Paul would be safe right now. I berate myself for not protecting Paul.

I sit there taking this in, gripping the hotel comforter with my hands. I feel like my heart is breaking again. I cannot find my breath. The words are hard to say, but I have to ask the question.

"Did you know who took John and Paul? Do you know where they are?" I plead into her eyes across the room. I need to know. I feel like I am on a different planet, removed from this world where happy people were still strolling down the street and going out for dinner with their families.

We can hear the tourists out in the hall. They are laughing and sharing stories from their day of sightseeing. Clouds pass by the window, sending dark shadows across the walls of room. Someone from housekeeping walks by and is talking in the hallway, but it all feels like white noise. I look down at the bed spread, inspecting its pattern, and hold the cover in one hand like a security blanket. Time seems to tick by very slowly as I wait for Jane's answer. I did not realize I had been holding my breath, and the world around me came back into focus. My grip loosens on the bedspread.

"No, Stella. I do not know who took your family. I did not have enough proof to even bring John in. I was close, but we needed more. John is an American hero, a decorated army officer. No one wanted it to be him. We think he was being blackmailed in the beginning, as part of an assignment he was on from Ft. Bragg that had him undercover in Morocco." Jane stops; I see her hesitate about divulging the rest of the story to me.

"Jane," I demand, "you have to tell me, I need to know."

"There is a woman from Morocco," Jane tells me.

"I know, her name is Rain. I found a note and receipts," I state flatly.

Jane nods her head *yes*. I think she is impressed I know of John's affair. Jane continues with the story.

"John and Rain developed a relationship while he was undercover there. They met two years ago. They had a child together, a little girl." I did not know about the child. My heart dips a little more. The gut punches keep coming.

"Essentially, John's lover, Rain, became like his wife in Morocco over the last year, and he joined her family; her father is part of a network from Jordan that John had been collecting information on. This group of businessmen supply guns to terrorist organizations and rogue nations. John's relationships are one of the reasons I believe he is our traitor." Jane's facts make my heart hurt.

Jane continues with her talking points.

"With Steve's help, I have pieced together a plausible account that if John's infidelity with Rain and their subsequent child got back to the unit, his career would be over both in the army and as a Special Forces elite officer. Steve has really been a big help to me, and he made me understand that John had developed a relationship with Rain, and he became a father to their daughter, Dove. I am sorry, but it is my professional opinion that your son is a casualty of his father's mess."

Jane's story is a lot to take in. It throws me a little that she mentions Steve's help multiple times. Her version explains so much. My hands grab more of the blanket, curling into fists. My mind whirls. I recognize a new emotion coming over me. I am furious at John. All of this chaos is because John kept a secret life with Rain and Dove. He put Paul and me in danger.

My beautiful son is a casualty of his father's mess. My son is missing because my husband is a liar and a cheat. Worse, he is a traitor. A liar, a traitor, and a cheat. The words feel like a rhythm being burnt into my soul. They repeat in my head over and over.

The crushing sadness has been replaced inside me with a cauldron of anger.

I take a large gulp of air and wipe the tears that had formed earlier when I asked about John and Paul's safety.

I sit back and close my eyes. It is a lot to hear and digest. John has a daughter named Dove. When would the stomach punches stop coming? When would my life stop exploding in front of me? I run for the bathroom. My dinner is not going to stay down. The drumbeat running through my body is making me sick.

It is like a poison striking my organs. My heart, my head, my lungs, my stomach, all of me is being attacked. I sit back on my heels in the bathroom and wipe my mouth with a hotel towel.

I sit down on the cold tile of the floor, the words in my head pummeling me over and over. The affair, the cheating, the woman, the illegal dealings, the secrets, John has a daughter, my son, my son, my son. It keeps circling me, robbing me of all other thoughts, making it hard to be aware of anything else in the room.

I look up from my trance to find Jane standing in the doorway, watching me as if I am a small child who needs rescuing. Watching is too mundane to describe what Jane is doing, because even in my I state I can tell she is tense and alert. She is watching for someone or something, gauging my reaction like she is tabulating a computer model to see what I will do next. Like Agent Scott, she has questions.

I realize that Jane has told me this story to gauge my reaction, to see what I know about John and his secret life. Jane wanted to know if I knew about the affair, about Dove and about the guns. Most importantly the guns. I cannot stay in this room anymore.

"Jane, I need to get out of here," I grab my purse off the bed and head for the door. "I need to clear my head and go for a walk."

Jane stands in front of the door.

"Stella, I don't think that is a good idea."

"I do not care what you think." I push her aside and open the door. I am surprised she lets me go until I notice she is on my heels following me. I have to wait for the elevator, so I do not get very far. I think about what she said.

I had pretended John and I were going through a bad patch in our marriage, a small bump in the long road of happily after, but deep down I knew something more was wrong. I did not want to admit it, but Jane's words make it impossible. My marriage is over. John is not having some small affair that he can end, and we can go to counseling over. He fell in love with another woman and had a child. They have been playing house. No amount of yelling, fighting and making-up can bring us back from this…even if I wanted him back. It is funny, but he has been gone from my life so much it was like he was already gone.

"Thank you for telling me this," I tell Jane, my voice coming across clear and much more business-like than I felt. Jane stands straight, nods her head, and smiles at me approvingly.

I stand there and walk back down the hotel hallway to my room ignoring the opening elevator with more calmness than I feel. Going back to the room, I stand in front of the window, reflecting on my marriage. The sun had set over the city outside my hotel room window. I take a deep breath and contemplate the last few years of my marriage with new clarity. My life was agreeable before this week. I did not have too much to complain about. All things considered, it seemed better than most people's lives. Looking back now, I see I didn't want to rock the boat to look too closely at the flaws.

Deep down, I realize I had wanted more in my marriage. I mean I wanted more than more sex; I was missing a connection with John. I never really had the courage to talk to John about the things that bothered me. A sigh slips pass my lips as I twirl the tassel of the drapes. A thought springs into my mind. *John has a daughter. I have always wanted a daughter.*

I am not surprised John had an affair. Over the years and all the deployments, sometimes I had wondered about it happening, one of us slipping up. I had watched a lot of couples we knew go through an affair. I thought we had been the lucky ones.

In military life, it happens all the time. Marriages fall apart. It is funny, after all the years I thought we were so superior to all of that. I would hear the other wives gossiping about that wife or that new girlfriend and feel so above them and thankful for my husband, for my perfect marriage, for my good husband. Here I am, actually one of them. Hell, John is worse than all those bad husbands put together. If you add the affair plus the daughter and the gun running. Out the window, I watch a couple walking down the street holding hands. I wonder how their story will end.

I am heartbroken. A sadness fills me for the loss of the picture of my marriage that I had created, that I am losing the life we had created together, that I am losing John and Stella, the couple.

It is as if the picture frame on my wall is tilted slightly off and I had not noticed, and Jane has come and straightened it out for me. So many things make sense now. I am disappointed in the woman I was who did not know that her husband was ruining their life. I want to hit John, throw things at him, yell and scream at him for destroying everything and endangering our son.

Fury rushes in, flooding through me like a storm. I make my hand into a fist, clenching and unclenching it, wishing I could hit something. I had done nothing wrong. I heard it takes two to break up a marriage. I feel the blood pumping through my veins. John screwed us up all on his own, the bastard! Anger is creeping into me, and it feels good. It is like an adrenaline rush pumping through my veins. My hand hits the window.

Bamm!

I am not responsible for any of this.

"*Damn him!*" bursts from me, exploding like a top under pressure.

I am feeling unhinged. I did not ruin our perfect life because I did not buy enough ice. John did it. He has destroyed everything. The realization, the relief of letting go of the guilt I have been carrying since Monday is more than I can handle. The emotions spill forth.

I have been on a bizarre roller coaster since the explosion. This new revelation has not broken me. I am not curled into a ball, trying to hide from this truth. I am not crushed and crying on the floor for my marriage anymore. I take a deep breath. I am fine. I stop clenching and unclenching my hand.

I am fine.

John chose to start a new family and it ruined him. I am not the same women as last week. I am stronger, tougher. I have been through a lot.

I look over to find Jane still observing me from the corner of the room.

A few tears escape my eyes, and I wipe them away with the back of my hand. I feel like I am not crying for the end of my marriage, but for the end of the life I had been working so hard to keep together. I tell Jane I am bushed and want to rest. Jane says that she has questions for me; that is why she is really here. She is still trying to track John and the shipments of guns, and she thinks I know more than I think I do. I do not want to talk. I need to do the opposite of talking about John and guns. I let her know we can talk in the morning. I don't care about the guns, only finding my son.

I crawl up to the pillow at the head of the bed and lay my head on the pillows. Jane says she will stay and settles into the chair. I lay on the bed and consider everything she has told me. My mind works through the story she laid before me like a picture book. Starting with John and I getting married. Paul being born. Our moves across the country through John's career and our last move to Fayetteville. All of it, until the morning of the party. I try to fit John's new story, his new wife and daughter and his misdeeds into my timeline, thinking back to John's deployments, his time away, things I had missed or did not want to see. It is too much for one day. I quickly fall asleep thinking of Paul and praying he is okay.

Chapter 16

I open my eyes as the sun filters through the window of my hotel room. It is Monday morning, one week after our Memorial Day pool party. One week ago, was the event, the explosion, where John and Paul went missing and changed my life forever. Lying on the bed, glaring at the ceiling, I think about the last seven days; I think about the last sixteen years married to John. I wonder what I missed being the super supportive wife of a military man. I always put John and Paul first; maybe, that was a mistake. With my marriage crumbling around me, I wish I had taken more time for me, maybe gone back to school and gotten a nursing degree. I thought we were happy up until recently. I reflect on John's behavior at the pool party; *how did I miss the signs of his affair?* It is hard to imagine that it has only been one week. I do not feel depressed or sorrowful anymore. I feel alive. I touch the area above my heart, stroking the heart necklace that Paul gave me for Mother's Day. I feel like my inner warrior has awakened and I am ready to defend myself from all the chaos that has entered my life.

It is hard to explain to myself; it is as if I had decided to change and, overnight, I did. I review the facts. According to Jane, John is a criminal, and I can do nothing about that. I lay there in the hotel bed, recounting Jane's story. After a few minutes of recounting some of the more painful details of Jane's story like the existence of Dove, I quietly slip out of the bed, putting my feet firmly on the soft carpet, and head to the bathroom to get changed. I am not ready to wake Jane. I need to meditate on what I had learned before I answer her questions. The one thing I like about this hotel room is that it has a nice big shower. I strip off my badly wrinkled slept-in new clothes and turn on the shower faucet. Opening the glass door and stepping in, I enjoy the hot water caressing my body. I let it glide down my back, washing away all of my unpleasant thoughts about John.

I reach for the soap. I have always liked a good shower to clear my mind and make me feel better. As I soap up, I let ideas about my future roll through my mind's eye. It seems that I am ready to think about my future. I shave my legs and enjoy the steam that has accumulated in the bathroom. It is like a fog that covers the glass doors. I slide my finger down the glass thinking about how I move forward from all of this. I finish washing my hair, step out, and dry off. I grab the fluffy white hotel robe on the door, and I wrap it around myself. I wipe the steam off of the mirror and brush my teeth with my new red toothbrush. I look at myself in the mirror. So much has happened in the last week. I mull over the fact that last week at this time, Monday morning I was lying in bed thinking about sex with John, that I sent John a text message to get his attention and have him come back to bed that I was hoping with one act that we could reconnect and solve all of our problems. I had been so naïve. I grab the hair dryer and review what Jane shared with me last night and all that had happened to me since the Memorial Day explosion. With my hair dry, I hurriedly dress and pack my things. I look around the room. Jane is waking up from her spot in the chair. Together, I know we can find Paul. He is out there, and I am not going to find him sitting around here feeling sorry for myself in some random hotel room.

"Jane, I am ready to go," I say. She slept in the chair and has not showered. I am way ahead of her. "I want to go to your office and figure out what our next steps are to tracking down Paul and John. At this point, I will go anywhere in the world and do anything to make sure my son is safe and home with me."

"My car is here in the hotel garage. Can you call down and get them to bring it around while I get myself together?" Jane slowly stands up and heads to the bathroom handing me her valet tag.

I walk over to the black hotel room phone and call downstairs, letting them know that we need Jane's car, and I will be checking out.

Within minutes, Jane and I head down in the elevator. In the lobby, I head to the front desk to check out, and Jane walks to the valet to reclaim her car. I turn around to find Jane being helped to her car by three men dressed in black suits. Two of the men are on each side like they are holding her up.

I freeze. What am I going to do? They are leaving with Jane. The old me would have yelled for help, but the new Stella knows I have to handle this before things get out of control. I approach the group and have an idea. One of the men is standing by the driver's door while the other two are working to get

Jane in the back seat. I walk to the man standing alone and greet him with a big kiss.

"Hello, love, thank you for waiting for me," I say out loud for everyone in the drive to hear. I start to kiss him like I am teenager making out in my parent's basement. The men are dumbfounded and taken aback. I take advantage of the confusion, and I kick the driver in the groin. I push him to the side, the element of surprise working for me.

Jane throws herself into the back seat, elbowing and kicking the men on her way in. I start the car and stomp on the gas as I close my car door. Jane is scrambling in the back seat to catch the door and right herself. I am focused on the road as we pull out into the busy Monday morning streets of D.C.

"Stella that was fantastic, quick thinking," Jane says above the roar of the engine and the traffic. I slow for a red light and see a sign that says, *Highway Next Right.*

"Jane, what did those men want?" I ask.

"It was funny. They thought I was Colonel Steve's wife, my cover. They must have seen me with you and assumed I would be good leverage to help them find the missing guns like when you were kidnapped," Jane tells me as she moves to sit-up.

More bad men looking for the cachet of guns. I start to wonder how come they all think I know something about these guns. Who led them to my family, to my home?

"How did they find me?" I ask.

"I think that when you used your bank account yesterday to buy some clothes, you alerted more than me to where you were."

Everyone wants those frickin' guns!

I pull onto the highway heading south. I look at my wedding ring shining at me from the steering wheel in the morning light. I curse John in my head reasoning that he brought this chaos to me. Jane climbs up into the passenger seat next to me.

Once we are away from the city, traffic starts to die down, and I focus back on what happened back at the hotel.

"Jane what is going on? Why are these men tracking me?" I am waiting for her to tell me more about John's operation and betrayal.

Jane is quiet for a minute and then comes clean. She clears her throat and starts her story, "When I went undercover as Steve's wife, we started spreading misinformation and bad intel to the unit, hoping to flush out the person selling secrets. We also were able to misdirect and take over two shipments of guns that John had going to criminal organizations in the last few weeks. Along with that, we put out that our mole in the unit, essentially John, was working with someone stateside. We made it seem like you were his partner—you were a husband-and-wife team, Bonnie and Clyde running guns and selling secrets from your home in Fayetteville. We were trying to bring everything to a head and flush them out."

"You purposely put my son and me in danger? *and*…told criminal elements that I was a criminal?" I exclaim. My voice booms off of the front window of her car. I cannot believe this.

"As the saying goes, sometimes the good of many outweighs the good of the few, Stella.

"That is a fact. We would not have come to your door if John was innocent. Steve helped me gather a lot of evidence on John. A big part was tracking his non-army related trips. John put in for a lot of leave recently. Steve really understood how important this case was to me and went above and beyond to make sure I had grounds for this," she states coldly.

"What…so that makes this last week of my life okay? My son is missing, my life is torn apart, I could have been killed by the intruders looking for guns, my home is burned down, I could have been assaulted by my kidnapper, but you have a lead on your bad guy, and I am supposed to be okay with that?"

I am upset and I am responding loudly to Jane's words. Jane and the CIA used us as bait. I see now that John did not have guns in our home, the CIA decided to tell the world that and now I am a target. My mind is circling. Jane is probably right about John being the match that started this inferno and brought chaos into my life. I try to redirect my anger at John; however, right now, I have enough anger to go around. I stew quietly and drive. I cannot believe Jane did this to me, to my family, to Paul.

Chapter 17

A few miles on the highway and I pull over into a highway rest stop in Maryland.

"You did good, Stella getting us away from those men. Quick thinking. Let's head south back through Washington D.C. to where my office is located in Virginia."

Jane's tone is condescending, but I shrug it off. It's been a long week, and I am not up for a petty squabble today. I don't really want to talk Jane at all since without her broadcasting information about the guns at my home I would not even be here. I miss my home. I miss my family. I mis my son. I try to find a positive in all of this chaos. What I really want to do is punch Jane or leave her here, but I feel like she might be my only lead to finding Paul.

"Okay, hopefully we can put our heads together with your team and find Paul when we get there," I say as I head inside the gas station.

Jane follows me and continues to talk. She seems chattier today, like we have become friends. I want to tell her we will never be friends. Frickin' Thelma and Louise!

"I knew I could trust you from the moment I met you at your party, especially after the explosion. I could tell after listening to your answers to the investigation team that you were not involved with John's activities. I have been working on this case for almost five years. Some of my colleagues were still not sure and wanted to keep an eye on you to see what you would do next, but I am close to this one…Stella…catching John means a lot to me," Jane reveals casually as if she is commenting on the color of the sky.

I can tell by the passion in her voice that this case is important to her.

We grab a few bottles of water and a bag of chips for the road. We switch places and Jane drives us out, pointing her car south.

She glances at me and begins to speak in a quiet voice, holding the steering wheel with both hands at ten and two like a new driver. She is going to tell me a secret.

"Five years ago, I was on assignment with the army. I spoke a few languages and was made the liaison to General Lightening Leonard Manoriski. I was young, and this was my first big assignment. We were headed to a peace keeping meeting. I was with the general in his vehicle. We were in Afghanistan in a convoy that took heavy enemy fire," Jane sounds as if she is looking through old pictures, reviewing what happened, and resolutely keeps her eyes on the road and hands on the steering wheel. Her voice is calm, and she stays very still. The quiet in the car is unnerving. I watch the passing cars and road signs waiting for her to resume. "Of course, this incident did not make the news. This is highly classified, but I need you to understand how much is at stake for me," she beseeches me and grips the steering wheel tighter.

"The military SUV in the lead of our convoy was hit with an RPG. It did not stand a chance. Our SUV was surrounded by rebel fighters. We had to call in an air strike on our location. We could not allow the general, as the face of our peace negotiations, to fall into enemy hands," Jane announces this as if she is sharing her favorite casserole recipe, not talking about death and war. Her story is incredible.

"Wait, Jane!" I cry and grab her arm. "Let me get this right. That means you told them to bomb your location; to kill all of you!"

Confusion and surprise race through me as I look at Jane. My mind is spinning with the implications. I shake my head no, that could not be what she's telling me.

"Yes, that is correct, Stella. My team died that day," Jane replies with no emotion. I look at her with new eyes.

"The order was given, and the missile was released. Everyone on that grid point was supposed to die that day, at that moment. There were to be no survivors."

Jane stops talking, and I am unsure of what to reply.

What do you say when someone tells you they almost died in an airstrike? Sorry for your loss?

After a few minutes of watching the passing trees and rolling what Jane dropped on me around in my head, I want to ask a few questions. My curiosity is getting the best of me. I need to clarify what Jane meant.

"Everyone?" I ask incredulously. "But you are here in this car with me?" I sound irritated. "This does not make sense." I run my hand through my hair. Jane takes a breath and looks at me like I am a misbehaving child.

"Stella, I will try to explain. After the missile detonated, a team was sent into recover what was left and make sure to clean up after us, making it look like we were never there. For some reason, my body was intact, and I was technically still alive, but barely. They flew me to the CIA facility in Virginia where we are headed now. The gun-runner at Ft. Bragg, your husband John, is the one I hold responsible for my trauma. Through my investigation at Ft. Bragg these last few months with the help of Steve, I mean, Colonel Whitman, I have uncovered that the gun-runner has been linked to the selling of classified information and details on troop movement."

Traffic is picking up, and it appears that Jane is done with her bombshell disclosures for now. I want to ask a question, but I am not sure where to start.

"My personal mission since that day has been to apprehend the person that did this to me and my team. I feel I am one of lucky few who have a second chance; a chance to make their destroyer face what they did." There is a force and passion in her voice that she has not demonstrated before. "Stella, I truly believe John is the traitor who gave up our location and got my team killed that day."

Jane's words shock me. Maybe, I should have seen this coming. I have nothing to say. My husband killed a team of soldiers for money. I suddenly understand why this is important to Jane. I cannot forgive her putting my family in danger, using my home and family, but I can see she is searching for a conclusion to her ordeal. Jane's closure is coming at a cost to us all. I wipe tears from my eyes. I do not know if I am crying for her or for me.

We pass a mom driving a minivan full of young boys. The boys look like they are watching a Spiderman movie on the backseat video screens. Paul jumps to my mind. I grab my heart necklace and pray for his safety. It is a little past three in the afternoon on Monday, about the time that Paul was taken last week. It feels like he has been gone forever. Sadness clouds over me, and I sit enveloped in helplessness and despair. My misery is punctuated by the thought that at least I have survived all of the insanity thrown at me, and I am still able to search for Paul. My heart is falling down a black hole of grief at my inability to connect the dots and find my son. All at once, I have a thought that is incongruent with my heartache of missing Paul and John's infidelity.

"Stella, Chris went off book by saving you at your house and then disappearing like that. He deserves an official reprimand. His actions were sloppy and inexcusable. I cannot say why he acted the way he did. I have not worked with him for very long, but I never would have jeopardized this case the way he did," Jane states professionally.

I contemplate the accusations that Jane leveled against Chris. I recognize he was saving my life, and I am grateful he went off-book. Without Chris there is no telling what would have happened to me back at my house.

"After you went missing, I went back to the CIA to report my findings and Chris's failure. Then I went in search of you, Stella. Chris should have reported in and told me where you were. His lack of communication has been a problem lately. Since his wife's death he has become withdrawn, isolating himself from the team. You were our only lead at that point," she sounds as if she is reading a report.

This lady is driving me crazy. I am her only lead? People were shooting at me, there were shots fired at me in my home and on the road in D.C., and she is upset because Chris did not file a report? "Can you blame him for not trusting the CIA. They kept his wife's death from him until he had finished his assignment. Work before family seems a poor motto, even for the CIA."

I think about Jane using us as bait for bad guys and my family being the only lead in a gun running case that caused my home to be burned down. I am infuriated by Jane's easy dismissal of Chris's heroic actions. I am grateful Chris stepped up when I needed him.

I go back to the part of Jane's talking points where she divulged that Chris had been kidnapped and beaten up. He had not abandoned me to Tony. I pray Chris is okay. My mind is a hive of activity. I have a lot to meditate on as I watch the passing landscape, the sedan quietly speeding along the highway. I hold my heart necklace and think about Paul. I pray he is okay. It starts to rain.

"Jane, the last I heard from Chris the CIA had learned that Paul and John had left the country in a private plane. Do you know anything more?" I ask hoping there is news.

"As of last night, I know that what we have found to be facts is that John is working with the gun-runners over in the Middle East. Actually, we are not sure if he is being held or working with them at this point. We can confirm that Paul is with him." Her answer gives me confidence that working with Jane will get me my son back.

As we roll through Virginia, I push the down button on my window in Jane's car. It slides away effortlessly, letting the fresh breeze into the car. It passes over me, and I enjoy the clean feeling. I reach my hand out the window and let it sway in the wind, catching rain drops. I remember taking car rides as a small girl with my parents in simpler times. I am upset with Jane for criticizing Chris for saving my life and trying to protect me, even if it didn't work out. Thinking back to everything that I have learned about John over the last few days, I realize it is not the one rain drop that hurts us. It is the thousands that beat down on us that catch us unaware that make us afraid of getting wet. The accumulation is what makes us run and hide from the rain, that makes us want to run and seek cover. We can only take so much.

I scan the road signs looking for familiar names. I gaze at the green pine trees and the blue-sky peeking through the clouds while black birds coast in the distance looking like they are circling up to the sun. The soaring birds are free of life's drama. They look like they can reach the heavens. I am envious of their peace. The air coming in the car smells green and new. I breathe in. The fresh air reminds me that I can survive this, that I am alive and still breathing. Through all that happened in the last week, I have prevailed. There is still hope I can escape this chaos. I recognize we are not far from the McDonalds that Chris and I stopped at on Wednesday on our drive up to D.C. I am like a hamster on a wheel, running in circles and going nowhere.

I roll-up the car window. I hang on to the fact that Paul is still alive; that is the best news I have had in days.

Chapter 18

We pull up to the CIA office in Virginia. The glass front of the rounded building reflects the impeccably cut, almost overly-green lawn and the well-spaced leafy trees lining the drive. The trees remind me of dominoes lined up or soldiers standing guard. This facility is made of clean lines, crisp landscaping and is, somehow, even sterile looking on the outside. I am reminded of a trip we took years ago to Disney World where everything is placed just perfectly to create a theme. Jane slows to a stop in the circular driveway at the white, marble front steps. I unlock my door and expect someone to come out to greet us, like a doorman at a hotel. I step out of the sedan and take in my surroundings. The is no breeze; the air seems very still, like we are in a bubble. There are no birds in the trees or squirrels hiding nuts in the grass. The sun is still up. I can see it setting over the trees. This CIA office seems custom made for Agent Jane Phoenix, perfect and strange. The rules seem different here.

I stand up straight and try to tame my hair with my hands. The front doors to the building sense our presence and open with a hushed whooshing click. They disappear almost like pocket doors or a magic trick, leaving a large, double-door sized hole in the mirrored brushed steel walls of the curved building. Jane comes around the sedan and stands next to me, waiting for me to say something.

"It looks like you guys have a great landscaper," I quip.

Jane frowns at me as I make a joke about her home. She directs me up the steps, like she is leading a small child into a school room. The only sound I can make out is our shoes as we walk on the white marble steps.

As we enter the lobby, I can hear calming, soft music playing—a summer orchestra with violins and flutes. I expect to see a fountain next and be offered some cucumber water like at a spa. The lobby is remarkable in its straightforward design. The marble steps give way to light-colored wood floors across the large room and are in contrast with all the glass, steel, and marble on the outside. On my right are two modern, wooden chairs that match the floor exactly, as if they were built from the same tree or had grown there like branches. The air inside smells sweet like at a fancy hotel such as the Ritz Carlton or Fairmont, where they pipe in scents to create a luxurious experience. I feel like I am supposed to be impressed by this place, but instead I feel like it is too modern, too weird. It is throwing me off-balance. There is no receptionist or lobby desk. I wonder if someone would come out to greet us or if anyone knows we are here. I feel very out of place. I speculate on how much this place cost to build. It is definitely a new office.

Jane adjusts her suit jacket. She is as unwrinkled as when I first saw her on Dupont circle watching me. Jane looks attractive, formidable and very tall. I am thankful to have my new clothes from one of the shops I had stopped in on Sunday afternoon in Washington D.C. I am wearing red capris with light-colored flowers down the side and a white, boatneck sweater with buttons on the sleeves. The flats that I had purchased to match the capris have black, red, and white flowers on them as well. We could not look more different. Jane looks like she is a secret service agent protecting the president, and I am a lady who lunches with the girls at the club.

Jane stands motionless, waiting for someone to come out and acknowledge us. I, on the other hand, cannot stand still. I move from one foot to the other, rub my hands and try to fix my hair. I am thinking about walking back outside and grab my bags from the sedan to give myself something to do when I hear soft footsteps coming toward us echoing across the lobby.

"Jane, I am going to—" I start to say, but my words fall off. Chris stands before me. My eyes widen, trying to take in what I am seeing. I thought Jane said he was at the hospital getting checked out after our encounter with Tony's men. I am surprised to see him here. I am glad he is okay.

"Stella, are you okay? Are you hurt? Did they hurt you?" Chris starts in. I cannot believe it is him.

I laugh out loud. We both start to talk at once.

"Hi," he says with a crooked grin.

"Hi," I respond like a teenager at a school dance.

"Stella, I told you I would protect you and I failed. Can you please forgive me?" That he cares is evident. I notice he has a few more bruises and scrapes than the last time I saw him.

"Chris, I—," There is so much I want to tell him. I feel like I have known Chris forever like we are old friends, instead of someone who came into my life a few days ago. I shiver I am not sure if it from the cold air conditioning or the look on Chris's face.

"You're cold, I think we should go for a walk outside while we talk it is nice out there." I easily fall in step with Chris, matching his stride as we step outside. We leave Jane behind I see her watch us go and turn and walk down an opposite hallway. The outdoor garden area of the building is beautiful. The sun is shining in the sky, touching the world with its rays, creating a rosy new day.

"Stella," Chris starts softly. "First, I must tell you, I am assigned to this case, your case to hunt for the person selling secrets at Ft. Bragg. Jane is working it from the inside, undercover, and I am on the outside, investigating and watching. You know from Jane that we believe that John is selling secrets and guns to some very bad organizations. Jane and I were assigned to hunt him down and put a stop to these illegal activities by any means necessary," Chris pauses. He emphasizes the last part. I can see he is working up to something big. "Stella, we have found John and Paul. They are alive, safe, and in New York City," Chris says forcefully.

My world turns on its axis. I feel like I am falling while standing still.

I am not prepared for Chris's bombshell. It is everything I have been praying for and, yet, I am at a loss.

I stop breathing. I reach out my hand to Chris to steady myself but stop and raise it to my mouth as his last words began to process. Tears fall from my eyes. Joy explodes in my heart.

Paul is found.

My prayers have been answered.

Paul is okay…it is a mantra. My heart beat.

I breathe out a long choking sigh and wipe the tears from my eyes. This nightmare that has lasted eight days is coming to an end. I look up towards the sun in the sky and lower my hand to my heart, reaching for my necklace. Chris remains in front of me as I process this announcement.

I take another deep breath. I have a mass of questions pinging around. Clearly, this is not what I had expected to hear this morning, and it takes a minute for me to absorb Chris's words.

"How did this happen?" I ask with a tremble in my voice. My emotions are spilling over. My body is shaking. I sit down on the nearest bench as Chris looks at me with sadness in his eyes before continuing to explain.

"From what we understand, John is involved with some criminal elements. What we did not realize was the lengths these evil men would go to in order to get what they wanted. On Memorial Day, last Monday at your house—from what we have been able to ascertain—when John and Paul went to the front yard, they were grabbed and thrown into a black cargo delivery truck. The team that took them then blew up the jeep in your front yard, wiping away all traces of their kidnapping. John and Paul were flown by private cargo plane to the Aden, Yemen in the Middle East and kept in a tent village where John was made to help them find a replacement shipment of guns in return for Paul's life. They felt John owed them, since the CIA—with information that Jane had gathered—had redirected the last two shipments of guns. These men needed John to make it right. They had paid for two shipments they did not receive."

My mind drifts back to Jane and my conversation yesterday. The CIA had worked out that John was the gun runner by stopping the shipments and feeding bad intel to the criminals, letting all doors lead to my home. The CIA's actions lead to my son's kidnapping. The intruders in my home that were looking for guns and threatened me were only there because of the intel being fed into the world by Jane and the CIA. The CIA facilitated a big part of the chaos that happened, that endangered us. Chris is still talking, and I try to focus on him.

"Eventually, John was able to thwart the plan the kidnappers had in place and escape with Paul." Chris stops and looks at me as if he is waiting for me to ask a question.

He starts to pace in front of me.

I think about what Chris revealed to me about John and his captors.

I know John is capable, he has been a special forces soldier for years. I do not doubt he could escape his captors. John has always been a good solider. I nod my head yes for Chris to continue.

"After John and Paul escaped, with the help of John's friend Rain, they flew home to Fayetteville where they found your home burned to the ground and you gone."

Anger courses through me. "They went to Fayetteville and I was off running around with you. I should have been there," I exclaim. Chris does not answer my accusation. He continues to tell me the facts they have collected.

"After traveling to Fayetteville, John and Paul met up with Rain and Dove in New York City. We have pictures if you would like to see them together.

"Stella, I want you to know I did think Tony would be the link to helping us find Paul. He is one of the gun smugglers that we know was used in this operation. I was sure he would give me evidence on John and Paul's whereabouts in return for his own freedom. I should have seen the double cross." Chris turns away from me.

The silence between us grows. I look up at the clouds passing overhead. They are moving slowly blocking the sun's rays from the garden.

Chris stands there waiting for me to say something.

…maybe to absolve him for…*for my kidnapping, for going to see Tony without back-up*…

I do not know what Chris wants from me. I am a cauldron of emotions boiling over anger topping the list.

Anger at the CIA for putting us in danger.

Anger at John for his illegal dealings that lead us here.

Anger at this person, Rain, who helped my family, who is with *my* family now and… Anger at myself for not finding Paul sooner.

Chris turns back around, gaining my attention, "Stella, let me be clear. John is in big trouble with the army and the United States government for selling secrets and guns. The case we are building at the CIA is coming together. Everything Jane found with the help of her contacts leads to John. What John did in the past hurt a lot of people. I hope you understand this is my job to get John," Chris says gently.

"We tracked John and the family…sorry for saying it that way Stella…our team followed them to New York City where it looks like they were making plans to start a new life," Chris continues.

Pictures of John and his new family walking in Central Park float into my mind.

I see Paul laughing and the family walking through the city. John and Rain eating dinner with the kids sharing an ice cream dessert. Things we would have done as a family except Rain is now in my spot.

Jealousy swamps me.

It is like watching a movie. I am torturing myself with these images. I do not even know what they are doing only that they have moved on without me.

I sit there sinking that in. My heart shifts.

I feel happy that Paul is safe, over the moon with joy. My son is safe. He and his father are going to be okay.

I would do anything to protect Paul. Over the last eight days that was all I was trying to do. Tears of joy course down my face.

Paul is safe.

My one wish is that I could have shielded Paul from the chaos and drama. The highs and lows of what Chris has imparted over the last few minutes are battling within me, converging at the same time. I recognize there is anger at John simmering too, but there is more joy that Paul is safe.

"I have to go to Paul. I must find my son and tell him I am alive. Paul is what is important."

I am trying not to focus on John being alive and the new little family he has created without me, my cheating military secret sharing liar husband who betrayed me, his unit, and his country. I will find a time to deal with him later. I don't want to think about Rain taking over my space in *my* family.

Right now, I want to find my son and give him a big hug. I need to get to New York City as fast as possible. I quickly walk back towards the building. Chris jumps forward and moves with me, seeing my urgency.

Pieces of my past life and of my past self, the woman who is always trying to please, to put on the perfect party to be the ultra-supportive military wife, these personas fall away, shattering.

I am a new woman. I am no longer hiding in my shell, waiting to be saved or trying to hide from the unwelcome facts. I have learned in the last week that I am a strong, smart woman capable of taking care of myself. I am no longer listening to the little voice in my head that is telling me I am not good enough, that if I tried harder John would love me, that John would want me.

That little voice had been wrong. I keep moving forward. I do not look back. I am on a mission.

My thoughts are all on Paul.

My son, my wonderful boy, my Paul is safe.

I am taking charge and going to get my son. My life is not perfect, but it is mine, and I want it back. I am ready to be in command! John better watch out. I am coming, and this is a Stella he has never met.

Chapter 19

I walk up to the building determined to confront John and save my son. I need to get to New York City as fast as I can. No more riding up and down I-95 feeling sorry for myself, looking for answers. John and Rain are setting up a new household with my son and starting their happy family. That is going to happen over my dead body.

John does not deserve to start over, I do!

I stop before the building, trying to figure out how to get the door to open. There must be a call button or a lever somewhere.

Jane walks around on the sidewalk and stands before me, stopping my exit from the garden. She looks at me imploringly.

"Stella, we need your help," she states passionately.

"I know that John is the guy we are looking for, the man I have been hunting, but we cannot prove it, officially, yet," Jane continues.

"What are you talking about?" I respond. I cannot believe what I am hearing, after everything they have put my family through, they need my help.

"I have learned in the last two hours that the team has gone through everything we have on John and we have no solid evidence against him. All we have is the word of a few criminals that he was working with them. That does not hold up in US courts. We could not even get a search warrant for the bank deposit box we found in D.C. It is the one attached to the account that FBI Agent Scott showed you."

"Wait, you fed the bad guys information on John and me and endangered my family on the word of a few criminals?" I exclaim.

I don't believe this.

I want to push past Jane and get going, this is ridiculous.

"Stella, I have been tracking this mole for years. I knew we were close," Jane is practically begging.

"Still, you directed criminals to me, and to my family at our home. I could have died if Chris had not saved me, John and Paul were kidnapped, and you had *no solid proof*," I shout at her.

I am incredulous. My words fill the quiet of the garden. This is too much.

"Sometimes you need to go with your gut," Jane claims resolutely.

"*Your gut!*" I am beyond mad. As if that solves everything. I am furious at her; at the CIA. They used my family.

What if they were wrong...?

What if they were right and the danger is still coming because of John?

There is only one way to find out. I need to help them. I need my family to be safe from this chaos once and for all. I focus on what Jane said about the bank account.

"What can I do? The account is not even in my name." I remember that the paperwork for the Wells Fargo account that Agent Scott showed me only had John's name on it.

"As a military spouse, we know you have a power of attorney for all of John's accounts," Jane states.

"Yes, John's unit has the guys update their paperwork every year. I got a new one in April, only a few months back."

"If you help us look into the box, I promise you, I will bring you to Paul," Chris interjects. He rests his hand on my back.

"Fine, we can go look into the safety deposit box," I agree hesitantly, "but if there is nothing there, we go straight to Paul, no matter what." I thrust my hand out for Jane to shake on it. It might look silly, but I need her word, no more delays.

Jane shakes my hand. I walk into the building with both Jane and Chris. I am not happy about agreeing to help them, but I feel like this is this is the best course of action to end this. The reality is that the CIA used my family. This fact is overwhelming me and making me want to lash out.

I want to rail at Chris, Jane, and the CIA for all the danger they let into my life and Paul's.

At least I know that Paul is safe for now. I hold on to my heart chain and think about Paul. *Let's get this trip to the bank in D.C. done. I need to reunite with my son.*

"Okay, let's get this show on the road. I want to see my son." My no-nonsense attitude is in full-force.

"Can Chris head straight up to New York City and keep an eye on Paul for us," I ask Jane. Let him use his special tracking skills to watch over my son, that is a good plan. I need to make sure I know where Paul is and that he is safe.

"Got it, I'll be on the next flight up there." Chris starts to walk away. Instead, he hesitates and stops next to me for a second. He looks like he is going to say something else, but instead continues on into the building to gather his gear.

I look over and Jane is texting on her phone and smiling like a teenager. "Who are you messaging?"

"Colonel Steve and I have become friendly," Jane answers.

"Here, let me drive. I want to get going and get this done," I state as I watch Agent Jane continues to text on her phone like a teenager.

Jane hands me the keys as she continues to smile at her phone.

"He says hi by the way." Jane starts as an opener looking over at me. I can tell she is trying to see if I am ready to talk.

"You told him I am here with you?" I ask her.

"Yes, I tell him everything lately. We have gotten really close since my time on Ft. Bragg playing his wife," Jane responds without looking up from her phone. She continues to talk about Steve and their plans to take a vacation next month after this case is closed. Jane talks all the way into D.C, I barely listen as I am focused on getting to Paul.

We pull into the parking garage at the Hilton Garden Inn on 14th street in D.C.

The city is filled with tourists. Families are everywhere, taking in the sites. We are only a few blocks from the White House. Jane and I walk down the street. She is wearing another navy suit and white blouse. It must be her work uniform when she is not undercover. The city streets are sweltering, the heat intensifies against all the pavement and concrete surrounding us. There is no breeze, and the air is baking me as we walk to the bank. I am dripping in sweat. The exhaust from the cars stuck in traffic is stifling. My nerves are catching up with me. Only a few days ago, I was walking in this area of the city with Chris before I was drugged and kidnapped by Tony. He wanted those guns so badly he was willing to trade my life for them. Since last Monday, how many times have I almost died? If I was a cat, I would be playing a dangerous game with my nine lives.

I spot a Potbelly Sandwich shop across from the bank, realizing I need a moment to regroup. I am a mess. I need to get my head straight before I go walking in there and asking for John's bank information. I can imagine that I am going to be arrested and hauled out like a common criminal if I walk in there a sweaty nervous jumble of crazy thoughts.

My mind swings, what if it is another trap like Tony or, worse. They could be waiting in the wings even now, ready to pounce and fire upon me. The thought of being taken again causes my hands to shake. I feel like I have barely had time to get all the drugs out of my system from the kidnappers and feel almost normal.

Less than 48 hours ago, I was in the room with the drunk who had his hands all over me. If I close my eyes, I smell his rotten breath on my face and his hand grabbing my breast. I have to stop my thoughts. I cannot revisit that episode, or I will lose my mind. I wipe the memory from my thoughts and replace it with the idea of stopping for lunch, something normal people do every day. I can do normal. I hold my hands together in front of me trying to calm my nerves.

"Jane, I am stopping in the sandwich shop across the street for a minute before we go in the bank," I say to her pointing across the street.

"Stella, I thought you wanted to get this done," Jane replies angrily. Now she is focused on the task at hand and off her phone. Still, I push for a break I need to be ready for this next step.

"I do, but let's make sure we are on the same page before we go in there." I need to get my head straight. Last week, I was worried about buying the right patio chair cushions and this week I am trying to outsmart gun-runners and human traffickers. It is all too crazy.

We wait to cross the street and walk into the restaurant. The air conditioning is on full blast helping to cool me down. I walk up to the counter and order a sandwich with extra peppers, bag of kettle chips and medium drink without asking Stella if she wants anything. The smell of food reminds me of my need to eat.

I watch the families passing by, missing Paul and John, too, if I can admit that to myself. A trip to D.C. is something we would have done as a family unit. Tour the museums, sit in the National parks, walk around the White House. I miss the idea of my family. It is hard to come to terms with the idea that John moved on. I know I am mad at him, but I am also sad for what I have lost. Losing a marriage after so many years is like the death of a dear friend or family member. I need to grieve for its loss, but I don't have time for that now.

My order comes up, and I find a small table by the window to sit down and eat. The food is tasty, and I devour my sandwich quickly.

I pull my iPhone out of my purse and pull up my emails, I had charged it in Jane's car. I remember getting one from John's unit on the power of attorney updates in April. I get lucky, and it comes right up. There is an attachment. I touch the square, and it opens the new document, signed by John, into a PDF on my phone. I have the document I need for when we walk into the bank. I take a screen shot of it, so I have it handy when we walk in, and lay my phone on the table. I have a hundred emails from friends and neighbors since I left Fayetteville with Chris. I do not want to look at any of them. I realize there have not been text messages from John or Paul. Maybe they have not replaced the phones yet. There is a missed call from Detective Johnson of the Fayetteville Police department and one from Agent Scott of the FBI both have left voicemails. I take a moment to listen to their messages. There is no new news on their end, would I please contact them as soon as possible. I think about returning their calls and realize that would only be wasting time at this point. Delaying helping Jane and getting to Paul. They are going to have to wait. I don't have time to catch them up on what is going on my case.

I am ready.

Jane has picked up her phone and is answering another text.

I have finished my sandwich, refocused, and am ready to go to the bank. I can do this; I can help Jane find evidence to arrest my husband. The thought makes my heart hurt. After almost sixteen years of marriage, it's hard to do this, even after everything John has done. I realize that does not make sense after everything I have learned about John and Rain. I tell myself this is the right thing to do. I need to control this situation and do what is right for Paul and me.

We leave the crowded sandwich shop and enter the mass of people on the street. Since we entered the city, the crowds have swelled by the hundreds. This summer in the city must be setting records for tourist dollars. We quickly cross the street and enter the Wells Fargo Bank. There is a young attendant, greeting customers as they enter. The bank is cool and bright. There is a line of people waiting for the teller.

"Hello, Welcome to Wells Fargo. How may we help you today?" The greeter asks.

"Hello, I need to get access to a safety deposit box," I reply.

The greeter motions for us to have a seat on the side of the lobby.

There is grouping of small red couches and a coffee table with current sports magazines on display. On the cover of one is a glossy image of a pitcher on the mound throwing a baseball. My heart lurches for Paul. My son loves baseball. I need to get him home, so he can play again.

Thoughts of Paul alleviate any unease I have at moving forward with Jane's plan. I need to get Paul free from the bizarre life his father had dropped us into.

"Have a seat here, and I'll let someone know," she states cheerfully as she walks away.

I can see the greeter type something into an iPad on her stand as she continues to greet new customers entering the bank. Two security guards watch the room from opposite sides.

The bank has piped in classical music to help set the tone. The music is slow and happy at the same time. I recognize a lot of flutes and string instruments. It reminds me of being at a wedding.

Jane scans the room, and I pull out my phone. I am reluctant to do this, but I am wasting time stuck in the bank. I scroll through the same friends and neighbors are asking for updates on John and Paul, on me and about the fire at the house. I delete them all. I am not sure what to say about any of it to people. How do I explain John's betrayal or being used by the CIA?

I am not even ready to let people know Paul is okay until I can see him for myself and give him a big hug. I cannot believe it has been eight days. It feels like a lifetime ago. The greeter walks over.

"Ma'am, I apologize. Mr. Thomas will be another five minutes. He is finishing up with another customer," she states as she looks at her watch.

"Great," I reply. "We can wait."

I look around the bank, inspecting the lobby. It is small, and I wonder why John choose this bank specifically. Why was he in Washington D.C.? A short, round man in tan slacks and a bank logo golf shirt walks towards us. His name tag reads Chip Thomas. He starts talking as he approaches us.

"Hello, I am Mr. Thomas. Jennifer let me know you need access to your safety deposit box."

"Yes, hello, I need access to a safety deposit box my husband opened here." I stand as he stops in front of us. Jane stands up next to me as if she is a friend.

"I see," says Mr. Thomas.

"Oh, I have a power of attorney, Mr. Thomas. Don't worry. My husband is in the army." He looks at me for a moment, assessing the situation.

"Thank your husband for his service, ma'am. We are all about helping our military families," Mr. Thomas replies with a smile on his face. I feel like I am in a commercial the way he is fawning over me.

"Follow me. Let's go to my desk and look up the account and verify your paperwork." He starts to walk to the side of the lobby. Jane and I follow in his footsteps and sit down across from him at his desk. I pull out my iPhone and my wallet, reaching for my driver's license.

"What is your husband's name?" he asks.

"John Evan Finch."

"And his date of birth?" He types into his laptop.

"November 8th, 1968."

"And his social security number and address?" Mr. Thomas finishes.

I answer the questions easily. The bank clerk looks up the account and information and prints out a form. He then asks to see my identification and power of attorney. I slide my driver's license and the PDF on my iPhone over to him. He inspects both and hands them back to me. I put my wallet and iPhone back into my purse. Mr. Thomas continues to type away on his laptop.

This is actually easier than I had thought. No wonder Jane wanted me to come with her and handle this. Jane takes out her phone, looks at the screen and hands it to me.

On the screen is a new picture of Paul.

He is wearing a New York Yankees T-shirt and blue shorts talking to a little girl on the sidewalk. He is smiling and happy. I have to admit he looks okay; nothing is wrong. The picture is so normal and such a blessing, tears start to well up in my eyes. I am overcome with emotion. I wipe my eyes and take a deep breath.

Paul is doing well. He is fine. He is safe.

I try to get my emotions under control. I look over at Jane and hand her back her phone. "Thank you…and thank Chris for me," I say quietly.

Mr. Thomas stands up and motions for us to follow him.

"Mrs. Finch, please follow me this way, our boxes are downstairs in the back." Jane and I walk quickly behind him.

"If your friend wants to wait up here," Mr. Thomas starts to say.

"No, she can come with me," I cut in.

We walk down a set of red carpeted stairs. The temperature grows cooler as we enter a vault.

"It is number 1538, on the right," he states.

He removes the box from the wall of metal boxes and places it on the dark brown wooden table in the middle of the room.

"I'll be at my desk when you finish," Mr. Thomas lets me know as he heads back up the stairs and out of the room.

I stand there watching the box like it might bite me. This is the moment of truth, when we find out if we have anything on John to help Jane's case. I cautiously slide the box open, removing the top, and lay it to the side.

Jane stands next to me, waiting.

The first objects I spot inside the box are a few pictures of Paul growing up and a folded letter addressed to Paul in John's handwriting on the bank's stationary.

Carefully, I move those on to the table. Laying the pictures side by side and the envelope next to them.

Next is a money clip with a red square on top containing a detailed raised green star decoration. The clip holds a number of one hundred-dollar bills.

John does not carry a money clip when he is home.

I place it next to Paul's pictures and letter. At the bottom of the box is a black journal with a lock on it and two dog tags etched with names on them that I don't recognize.

Jimenez and Smithton.

I reach in for the journal. It is small, like a teenage girl's diary, with an added feature, a circle key lock on the top that looks handmade. I inspect the journal while Jane picks up the dog tags.

"I know these names; these men were killed by the gun runners in the Middle East a little over two years ago. They were stationed at Fort Bragg. They were the part of the case that led me to Ft. Bragg and John's unit," she explains as she glides her fingers over the names on the tags.

I am half listening to her. I am contemplating the half-circle shape of the lock on the journal. It appears familiar. I scan the contents I have laid out on

139

the table. My eyes fall on my hand and notice my wedding ring. John and I have matching ones. We had them custom made, each ring has a square and a circle entwined on the top of the band. I take my band off and place the top of the band into the journal and turn it. It fits. The journal unlocks.

I glance over at Jane still holding the dog tags. This is what she has been waiting for; some kind of confirmation of John's nefarious dealings. The moment of truth is upon us. This journal could be the key to her case. The dimly lit safety deposit box room adds to the solemnness of the occasion.

Slowly, I open the black book to the first page. John's handwriting covers the page.

This journal is to document my assignment to investigate and find the person in the United States Army who is selling military secrets and guns in the Middle East. I am documenting my process because I know things could go sideways fast on this. It is a dangerous mission. I may lose my life before I complete it, as Captain Jimenez and Master Chief Smithton did. They got very close to figuring out not only the unit on Ft Bragg, but the identity of this criminal. This will be a long and arduous investigation for me and my family. It is important to note here that I have been assigned this duty by General Patterns of the Joint Chiefs and that I am to tell no one. That is another reason I am keeping this journal here in the bank under lock and key. Only two people will know I am working on this, myself and General Patterns. This journal is my safety net. I will be going undercover and moving my family to Ft. Bragg, North Carolina where they believe the traitor is stationed. For taking on this assignment, I will be given a bonus and extra hazardous duty pay, as I will be working as an army officer completing my normal duties and taking on a greater second task to identify the problem on Ft. Bragg.

This entry is dated a little over two years ago. I reread the page and tears start to fall. John is not the criminal.

John is not selling secrets and guns.

He is not evil. He was working on finding the bad guy. He is a good soldier.

My heart is uplifted. I almost want to laugh as the pain and uncertainty I have been holding in is released. My husband of sixteen years, the father of my child, is not a super villain. I reach over and share the first page with Jane, she scans the page and then I take back the journal. I am not willing to give it up I need to read what John has written. It is cathartic.

Jane goes to the corner where there is a chair and sinks into it. The implication of John's journal sheds new light on her investigation, her work for the last five years. John was working the same case. She puts her hand on her chin, thinking hard and staring off into space. Jane's gut had been wrong. She had sent the criminals after my family for no reason.

I flip through the pages of the journal, scanning them quickly. They document John's trips to the Middle East. The names of cities jump out at me as I remember these are the same cities that Agent Scott had asked me about back in the FBI office in Fayetteville. There are a few mentions of Rain, but I turn those pages quickly. I am not willing to read that part now. Towards the end of the journal, I recognize a name that catches my eye, Colonel Steve Whitman. I read the page.

May 15

I met with General Patterns at our usual spot in Washington D.C. to update my progress. I finally have a name to go with the secrets. I am sure of it. Colonel Steve Whitman. He is the senior officer of my unit at Ft Bragg, and this is going to get tricky, but I have proof. I have a picture of Steve meeting with someone in Riyadh, Saudi Arabia when he was not supposed to be there and an informant, who is a hotel owner, who is willing to testify that Steve has stayed in his hotel numerous times over the last five years. The witness has records to back this up. I think I have him this time, the traitor. I am waiting for the general to get back to me on our next move.

I stop there.

I can't believe what I am reading. Jane's fake husband. The man who helped her, who supplied her with intel and information on John, is actually the traitor. Colonel Steve who had come to our pool party overdressed, wearing the flashy Rolex. I think back to where Colonel Steve was when Jane stood next to me during my first hours with the investigators. He is not present in any of my memories of that day after the explosion in the front yard until Jane and he left. He was missing for hours. Maybe he was hiding purposely from the investigators, the FBI, and the Military Police, not wanting his name on any of the official documents. Not wanting to be asked questions about what happened. I think back to the intruder. He had said colonel. It was a not mistake. Even when I was kidnapped, I heard the colonel mentioned. Now, it all fits. They all knew they were working with a colonel...Colonel Steve Whitman.

I look over at Jane and she can see I am simmering with anger.

The man she trusted and collaborated with on this case, together they brought the evil to my home that day. They did this Jane and the colonel, together. My hands are shaking as I remember John's Jeep in flames in my driveway.

I flash back to Jane had explaining to me that she had leaked John's involvement and my working with him to the gun runners because John was the criminal. *She has told me John was the gun-runner!* The truth here runs through my veins like firecrackers going off.

She had admitted to opening us up to harm because John was not innocent. *NOT INNOCENT*. Explodes in my head.

I storm over to her and shove the last page of the journal in her face, making her take it from me. Jane starts to read.

I walk back to the table and pick-up John's letter to Paul. It is not sealed. I unfold the note to take in what he has written there to our son.

May 15 Paul,

I want you to know how much I love you and how proud I am to be your dad. I have been working on a special project for the government the last few years and have not been home with you as much as I would have liked. Don't think for one minute that my trips were a reflection on you. You are more than I could have ever wished for in a son.

If you are reading this, something has happened to me. I thought it was best I leave you a note. In my line of work, you never know if you are going to get a chance to tell the ones you love how important they are to you.

There is a bank account here at Wells Fargo that I have started for you as a college fund. There is not all the money you will need for tuition there yet, but I am working on it. When I go on these trips, the government gives me a stipend to cover expenses. Every dime I can save I have been putting into this account here for you. Now, I still think you will get that baseball scholarship; I am pulling for you. Think of this money as a safety net. Everybody can use one. If you don't need it for college, maybe use some towards a new car or a down payment on your first house. I wish I could be there for all those firsts to help you navigate the way. No matter what, remember how much I love you and that you mean the world to me. Never doubt that.

Now, I know I am asking a lot, but I need a favor. This one is going to make your mother angry, and I am sorry for that. If I am gone, there is someone I need you to know about. You have a little sister, Dove. She lives with her mother, Rain, in Morocco, and she is five months old and will need a big brother. I know you will be mad at me about this at first. You have every right but do me a favor through the years. Please check on her. She is your family, and it would mean a lot to me.

Take care of your mom. I know you are going to do great things with your life.

All my love,
Dad

I fold the letter and pick up the two pictures of Paul. One is Paul's school picture from a few years back, and the other is a picture of Paul playing baseball.

I drop the pictures back into the safety deposit box. I wipe the tears from my eyes.

John is a good dad.

He is saving money for Paul's college. He had made the extra money working hard for the government doing double duty so to speak. His regular job and then this secret extra assignment. I had doubted John's career and work integrity, and this makes me sad. It had been easy for me to believe the worst of John, even though we were only having what I thought was a hiccup in our marriage. As the FBI, Agent Scott, and CIA had stacked up the information against him, I had believed them. John's letter to Paul was the man I knew, the dad that carried Paul around our home dancing with him and singing him songs when Paul was a baby was not a lie. It is as if a weight has been lifted from my body.

I look over to Agent Jane in the corner. She still holds the journal, flipping back through the pages, reading every line. She is shrinking in her guilt. She knows she was mistaken about so many things.

"You were wrong; your gut was wrong…" I spit out at her.

"Yes, I can see that, Stella…I am sorry…I thought…I needed to find the person who let my team get killed all those years ago. I had worked so hard to find the person…I am sorry…I know I led the bad guys to your door. I did this…John was not… It says here John was…Steve was…I was so very wrong…" I can see the confusion in her eyes, but I don't care.

"You are the reason my life has been a living hell for the last eight days, that my husband and son were taken. *You*!" I shout at her. My voice is very loud in the small bank room. I am shaking with the anger.

"Stella, I apologize. I have nothing I can say, no defense that makes up for what you went though, for my bias in listening to Steve, to putting your family through all of this…I am sorry," she states running her hand through her short blonde hair. She stands up. "Steve was…I thought he…I thought we had something." She knows that is no excuse for what I have been through. "How could he do this to me? We had a special connection? We had plans for our future…" her thoughts trail off for a second. "I thought I was helping, taking control of the investigation, putting things in motion that once and for all would show me who the traitor was—that I could end this hunt. I did not know, I was trying to do the right thing to save more lives, more secrets from being sold." She walks towards me.

"You framed the wrong man, but you did it for the right reasons, is that what you are trying to tell me?" I wipe the tears from my face and press my fingers to my temples.

I am floored.

"Admit you were wrong, that Steve took you and played you like a fiddle. John was the one who solved this case, and in two years. How long have you been searching for the mole, four years, five?" I snap at her.

"I am never wrong. I am a good agent. John is the bad guy here. Steve is my guy. You and your family are the greedy criminals in all of this. Taking the money and living the good life. I have spent years on this case. I was sure John was our guy," Jane continues in her defense.

Something occurs to me then. Five years ago, John was not assigned to the Middle East. He had been working in Danville, Alabama teaching.

"Jane, did you even check where John was five years ago? He was nowhere near the Middle East. He had made no trips there. He was down in Alabama teaching. It was not until we moved to Fayetteville that he had started traveling

144

there and that was two years ago." I am shaking. The truth of this week is too much.

"Okay, you are right, maybe I was too quick to go after John, but Steve had all this evidence, and we were such a good team. Working together on this made so much sense. Everything pointed to John. This case was going to make my career.

"What did you do?" Venom drips from my every word.

Jane tries to calmly and logically answer me again even though I have backed her into a corner. Nothing she can say is going to help her now.

"Stella, I worked with Steve. He pointed out to me the soldiers in his unit that could be the ones. I ran their names through our data base, and John had a lot of trips to the Middle East. He seemed to have access to a lot of money. I admit it. I got excited. He had done one bad thing by having a second wife and child over there, it was straightforward to think he could do other worse things. It was easy for me to attach the rest to him as well. I can admit that now. I thought we had our guy, that I had finally made a connection after years of searching. I don't know what to say, Stella, I was wrong."

I look at the journal in her hand, John's vindication. I take it from her.

"You owe John, Paul, and I more than an apology; you owe us so much more than an apology." I am only inches from her face. I can feel her defeat. I can hear my anger. The room is too small to contain all of our emotions.

"Jane, we need to go and find General Patterns. John and Paul may still be in the danger that you brought to our door. Everyone thinks that John is a criminal."

I put the safety deposit box back together and drop the journal into my purse. Jane is moving slowly. All of the evidence she has learned here today has taken her out of the game, but I need her to pay attention. She is stuck inside her head, thinking back over all her bad decisions. I start to leave the room to get Mr. Thomas.

"Jane come on," I say back to her. She walks after me. Mr. Thomas is waiting in the hall.

"Thank you for your help today," I say to him as I shake his hand and move past him up the stairs. Jane is now following me.

"Jane, I need your phone," I bark at her as we enter the lobby. She hands it over.

I quickly look up Chris's number and hit the call button as I walk out of the building. Chris answers.

"Chris, this is Stella. John is not the bad guy. He and Paul may still be in danger. Jane and I have learned that Colonel Steve Whitman is the mole selling secrets. Chris, I need you to protect my family," I say quickly, my words rush together. I can get them out fast enough.

Chris responds, "Of course, Stella. Is Jane there with you? I will do whatever we need to do. That is incredible information you uncovered. Are you and Jane headed here?"

"No, I need to talk to General Patterns of the Joint Chiefs. He is the only one that can clear John's name and make this right." Energy is surging through me. I am excited to be sharing our discovery.

"Okay," Chris replies and pauses.

"That sounds complicated. I heard on the way up here that the Joint Chiefs are at the White House today for meetings on National Security. I don't think you will be able to reach him." I don't have time for Chris's negativity. I have let people control me and tell me what to do for too long.

I head down the street to the parking garage where we left Jane's car. I stop and turn around, getting my bearings. The White House is in the other direction.

"Got it, thank you." I hang up the phone.

I toss Jane back her phone. I need to reach General Patterns. What if some well-meaning FBI or CIA agent spots John and Paul thinking they are bad guys and tries to take them in? One of these good guys could open fire on my family and try to be a hero. The scenario sends chills down my spine. I have to do something to save them. We are so close to ending this and yet I feel on the verge of it all going sideways fast again.

I run my hand through my hair and stop the thoughts. I need to make sure Paul and John are safe. I stand on the street corner and think back to the journal. There was a phone number on one of the pages at the bottom. I pull it out of my purse and flip through the pages. Families and tourists' groups walk around us on the sidewalk. They are loud and excited to be on vacation. I cannot let them distract me. I find the page with the phone number, retrieve my phone, and dial.

"Hello?" a man answers.

"This is Stella Finch, Major John Finch's wife. I need to talk to you immediately," I say quickly before the person on the other side can hang-up.

"How did you get this number?" he asks.

"From John. It is urgent or I would not be calling." It is somewhat true that I got the number from John; it is from his journal.

"We can meet later today. I have meetings all day today," the man says.

"No, now. I can be at the White House in ten minutes. Can you meet me at the gate, General Patterns?" I say, remembering who I am speaking to. I pause, crossing my fingers and waiting for an answer.

He hesitates. "Mrs. Finch I will send out my assistant to meet you at the gate, a Captain Jones. I can give you five minutes," the general responds.

"That will work, sir, and I have Agent Jane Phoenix of the CIA with me as well, just so you know," I finish and hang up the phone. I bet it has been a long time since someone hung up on the General. I do not have time to worry about his feelings. I start jogging towards the White House.

Jane follows along with me as I fill her in. I am not wasting anymore time. I need to convince the general to get involved and clear John's record and put out a warrant for the arrest of Colonel Steve Whitman. I don't trust the CIA to arrest him since he has been working with them.

I grab Jane's phone and text Chris that we are headed to the White House to meet with General Patterns. He sends me back a thumb's up emoji.

Jane and I arrive at the side gate of the White House minutes later. There is a security guard gate house and Captain Jones is waiting for us. I introduce myself and Agent Phoenix to him. He hands us white lanyards with a big blue V on them, our visitor passes, and leads us to the security checkpoint. The White House security building looks like it was built in a hurry. It is sparse and missing a decorator. It reminds me of a hall you might rent for a wedding, a long rectangular building with windows overlooking the lawn of the White House. The process reminds me of TSA screening at the airport. They check my bag and Jane has to leave her gun. We walk through the x-ray machine and someone asks to check our identification. Jane produces her badge, and I take out my driver's license. Our names are added to a list of visitors allowed to enter the White House today. A clerk on a computer seems to be Googling us and doing a quick background check. It is a surreal moment; I never thought I would be visiting the White House, not in a million years, and not like this, for a meeting with General Patterns.

Once we are cleared, Captain Jones hurries forward out of the security building. I am fast on his heels. Jane is next to me. We enter the White House through a side door.

"General Patterns only has a fifteen-minute break between meetings. This break is happening right now," he looks at his watch as he dashes forward. "We are going to meet him in John Kelly's office, the chief of staff," he clarifies. "He is a friend of the general's."

I follow the captain through the corridors. I glimpse what I think is the first lady and a team moving down another corridor. I realize she is talking to her son. I think about Paul and hurry my steps.

I enter the office a few steps behind Captain Jones. He is a short guy, and I can see over his head.

I stop and take a breath.

I feel like everything…these last eight days has led up to this moment. I step to the side of the captain as Jane follows me into the office.

"Mrs. Finch, this better be good. We have important National Security issues being debated here today, and I have not even had any lunch yet," General Patterns exclaims as he looks at the clock on the wall. It is after 1pm. I look around the office and gather my thoughts.

"General Patterns, eight days ago, my husband, Major John Evan Finch, who works for you, and my son were kidnapped during an explosion at my home. It was instigated in part by the CIA because you did not share information with them that you were also conducting a secret investigation into the mole at Ft. Bragg. They, the CIA, thought John was their guy," I point at Jane. "Over the last week, I have been attacked, I have been shot at twice, my home was burned down, I was drugged by a Russian mobster and kidnapped. I think, respectfully, you can give me five minutes, sir," I state trying not to sound too dramatic, but I know my facts are unbelievable.

Captain Jones looks at me. I can see my words have startled him. This is no ordinary meeting.

The general speaks up, "Mrs. Finch I am not sure what you are talking about…how can I help you?"

I know this is a matter of national security and top secret, but at this point I don't care. I am not taking his denial.

"General, I am not playing games. I have your cell phone number from John's journal. This journal contains notes all about my husband's assignment that you personally set up, your private meetings on the progress of the investigation, and John's conclusions. Two years of information. I am willing to use what I have to stop this madness, but I would rather you did it, please, sir." I pray this works.

The general sits on the front of his desk and considers my statement. He is in his full uniform. He has aged well and is a formidable looking guy. I can see he could be a tough cookie. I am sure a meeting with him would be intimidating if I had not been through so much already. He looks from Jane to me.

"You work for the CIA and were working this investigation?" he asks Jane, pointing his finger at her.

"Yes, sir, I am Jane Phoenix of the CIA. I work out of the team at the Science Medical Technology Project in Virginia. My team and I have been hunting this traitor for five years."

The general crosses his arms. Captain Jones is watching the clock on the wall. "Okay, Mrs. Finch, what can I do for you?" He repeats, looking at the journal I am holding out in front of me.

"I need you to release a statement clearing John's name with the CIA, FBI, and all the government agencies that might think he is a criminal. I want you to let them know he was working for you and that he has done nothing against our government. Essentially, that he is one of the good guys, a hero before some young government agent gets him in his sights and takes a shot thinking he has caught someone bad, like Robert P. Hanssen. Then I need you to let the world know that Colonel Steve Whitman is the mole and traitor. He should be arrested immediately, before he hurts more people," I pause for moment looking him in the eye. "If you had done this two weeks ago, when John brought you the conclusion of his investigation, I think the chaos that has come to my life could have been avoided. Will you help me?" The words rush out like I am running out of time. My heartbeat has sped up as I think of John and Paul in danger, again. "I know I am asking a lot," I finish, thinking I covered it pretty well.

"Now that you bring this to my attention, I did have a missed call from John two days ago. I did not think much of it. I have been busy here at the White House, and he did not call back," the general states as if he is thinking over a problem. He looks at Captain Jones, "Well, you heard the lady. We need to release some statements interagency and get this ball rolling. I cannot have one of my best guys in danger out there. I apologize, Mrs. Finch, for everything you have been though. That is quite a story."

He gets up from the desk. Captain Jones replies to the general with a quick affirmation that he will get on this immediately.

"Thank you, General, I appreciate your help," I respond. The general gets up to walk out. "Excuse me ladies, it is bad form to keep the president waiting. The next meeting is about to begin." And he exits the room.

I watch him walk past us. I smile and laugh out loud. I cannot believe I stood up to a General. I grab Jane's arm. I close my eyes and say a little prayer.

When I open my eyes, Captain Jones is watching me.

I sink down into the chair in front of me. I look around the office, letting it sink in that I am in the White House. There are pictures of chief of staff with the president and his team on the walls. There are awards from his time in Marines.

Books are stacked on the cabinet behind the desk. This really is the chief of staff's office right hand man to the president. I am a few feet from the oval office; it is as incredible as everything else that had happened me in the last week. I am starting to see the pendulum swing in a good direction, maybe everything is going to be okay.

Yes, I can make this okay.

Jane is standing back behind Captain Jones. I think she is still in shock from being wrong, maybe for falling for the wrong man. I cannot help her with her guilt or her love life, but I need her to get back to helping me get to my son. She promised to get me to my family and that is where we are going next. I need to make it to Paul today and give him a big hug. I feel like I have got the chaos of our life under control now. My heart is soaring with happy news. I cannot wait to see Paul and get our lives back. We can move forward safe from all of this.

Chapter 20

Captain Jones turns out to be a really nice guy. He works to help us book flights on his laptop while simultaneously using the phone to circulate the interagency information on John and Steve. Jane and I thank Captain Jones for his assistance. It feels like I have made a new friend.

I run with Jane at a full-on sprint leaving the White House over to the Farragut West Metro Station to catch the blue line, leaving Jane's car in the parking garage by the bank. I am hot and sticky, but I do not care. I am on way to Paul. We barely make the flight, a Delta shuttle out of Reagan International to LaGuardia Airport in New York City.

As we take our seats, Jane tries to apologize again for using my family as bait, but I ignore her. I take the window seat on purpose, turning my body away from Jane. I need to think and sort out my emotions. They have been running a hundred miles a minute since the bombshell at the safety deposit box. John's journal blew Jane's case out of the water. All of the so-called facts that I had believed about John were an invention of Colonel Steve Whitman's sick mind. His need for power and money, his greed almost cost me everything.

To be honest, I am feeling overwhelming guilt at how easily I was led to believe that John masterminded evil across the globe for money. I feel like such a fool. I was easily pulled along on this mountain of fake accusations that were piled on my family. I was so self-righteous about putting away a criminal, my husband of almost sixteen years. Sure, we had grown apart, but I am floored that I could easily believe he was a gun runner and seller of military secrets.

The revelations from the journal comfort me. John is not responsible for killing innocent people, and I am not married to a monster. John committed infidelity and ruined our marriage, but he is not a criminal. There is some strange consolation in that fact. I almost feel relieved at the journal's disclosures. I can take solace in the truth that in his career, my husband, Major John Evan Finch, is a good man, even if he is not a good husband.

The flight attendant stops by to ask if we would like any beverages and hands me a pack of pretzels. I opt for a glass of ice water. It's not the most exciting option, but I am in a complicated mood. I need time to think.

I open the pretzel packet and lay the snacks out on my napkin. My hands are shaking. As I eat them one at a time, my life scrolls before my eyes.

A week ago, I was worried that John and I were not having enough sex, that our marriage had lost its passion. Now, I sit on this plane, realizing that I have lost my marriage. It is almost laughable. Before our pool party, I was worried that John did not like the flowery patio chair cushions on the back deck. Today, I realize that none of that mattered. It is amazing how being marked as a criminal can put your life in prospective.

I eat another pretzel. *One the one hand, Yay! John is not a criminal. One the other hand, What the hell? He is such an asshole! He is a cheater and liar.*

I drink some of my water and contemplate the growing clouds outside the plane.

I rotate two broken pretzels on my napkin. Each is missing a side, so I push them together. They are not the same and do not fit together as I feel they should. They can never be one perfect pretzel. I pop one of the broken pieces in my mouth and realize that it is stale.

How could he cheat on me!

I am furious at John.

I am getting a divorce. Our marriage is finished!

I crush the remaining pretzels into my napkin and drop them into my empty water cup with my napkin, wiping the dust from my hands.

I spin my wedding rings around my finger examining them from all sides. I slip them on and off my finger. Finally leaving them off.

As we land, Jane checks in with Chris on her phone. He lets us know that John is staying in a suite of rooms at the Peninsula Hotel on Park Avenue. They are registered under Rain's name Chris has booked me a room there as well. We leave the airport and catch a taxi. The temperature in New York is a few degrees cooler than D.C., but it is still hot and humid.

"Jane," I ask as climb into the car, "how is John affording a suite of rooms on Park Avenue at the Peninsula? That sounds expensive and very fancy even with the extra money he is making working for the general."

She looks over at me. "I must have forgotten to tell you that Rain inherited wealth from her mother's side of the family. It is all totally legit, unlike her father's businesses. All the money around John was one of the reasons I thought he was our traitor. Obviously, I was wrong about him selling secrets and guns for money. I want you to know that I feel terrible about everything," Jane continues to talk about her mistakes in the case. I look out the window at the passing cars. I think about Jane's admission. Not only has John replaced me with Rain, but she has money. Not just money—wealth, like she is the fricking Queen of England. I try not to be mad about that, but I feel the knife twisting in my gut.

How nice for them.

I like to think I am good person, but not hating Rain is more than I can manage at this point. Plus, I am not ready to forgive Jane for bringing all the madness to my door.

Our taxi has a television anchored to the back of the front seat. It is playing highlights of a young hip hop star asking his model girlfriend to marry him on stage at Madison Square Gardens. The host is gushing about their cuteness. The story gives me the urge to punch something, and I hit the off button with force.

Chris is waiting for us on the sidewalk as we pull up to the hotel. I realize Jane had been texting him our progress.

This is definitely a hotel for royalty. The twenty-three-story building seems like it is pulled straight out of a classic movie on AMC. I am sure celebrities stay here. John and I would never have splurged for something like this during our marriage. The thought makes me mad. We would have opted for the Doubletree or Embassy Suites since they come with breakfast included during your stay. Always trying to make John happy, that was the old Stella.

I am sure Rain never worries if breakfast is included.

I look around the lobby again. I half expect to see Julia Roberts coming down the stairs to meet Richard Gere as they head to his jet and the opera. I am sucker for Pretty Woman. I need to focus on why I am here. This is not a vacation or an episode of Lifestyles of the Rich and Famous. I need to get out of my head and put away my heartache.

"Chris," I turn to face him, "where is Paul?"

"In the pool area on the 22nd floor. They are all up there enjoying the sunshine and warm weather. The four of them had been out shopping down the street at a department store. I observed them from a distance grabbing lunch earlier at Five Guys. I have not seen anyone else tailing them or monitoring their movements," Chris states as if he is giving us his report.

His accounting of their whereabouts sounds incredibly normal, family-like, and reasonable. It makes me anxious to see my son, to reconnect as a mom. I am jealous of their normal day.

I scan the lobby as if I can spot a bad guy popping out behind a vase of flowers.

My life would be easier if it was a video game with signs over everyone's head telling me who they are and what their mission is. I spot a gentleman crossing the lobby in a crisp black suit, a definite James Bond type. I am sure the bad guys are lurking, ready to pounce and take my son from me again.

"Let's head up there first." I need to see Paul with my own eyes. I start forward. Jane and Chris both nod, and we head to the elevator. The ride takes forever.

Unexpectedly, I am nervous when the elevator reaches the pool area. I step off and walk onto the glass-enclosed floor looking for Paul. I spot him across the room standing next to a small baby girl she can barely stand, and Paul is helping her move around the pool. That must be Dove.

Paul sees me as I approach. I notice John and an exotic-looking woman coming towards me as well. I quickly continue towards Paul. He rushes over to me and wraps me in a tight hug. It is the best hug ever.

"*Mom! Mom!*" he sounds like he is five again, repeating my name. The relief of seeing my son engulfs me in an overpowering rush of emotion. I step back, and my clothes are soaked, but I do not care. My son is safe. My smile could not be bigger. I am overcome. I keep Paul close.

"Let me look at you."

I run my hands around him, looking for bumps and bruises. There are none. My son is perfectly fine and has a story about an amazing adventure. Paul sounds incredibly happy. I wish I could say the same. The best part of this is hearing his voice say "Mom." There were times over the last eight days that I thought I would never hear that again. I try to keep my perspective. We are all alive. There are things to count as blessings.

"Mom, we went to Fayetteville, but the house was burned down. You were gone. Dad was making calls, but we didn't know what happened to you. He thought you were in Washington D.C. because someone used your card, but when he called you had checked out. I don't have my phone anymore," he continues without taking a breath.

Paul is jubilant and excited to share with me. He is not acting like a teenager at all. "Dad tried your phone a few days ago, too, but it was turned off…" Paul trails off as his dad approaches us.

John holds his hand against Rain's back as they approach. The warm and thoughtful gesture makes my heart drop. Even though I knew about them, I am not prepared for the sight. It hurts like I have been punched in the gut. I am angry at John. I want to scream at him, but I also want all of this to be over. I am resigned to what comes next. I know I have no choice. My eyes drop to the black tile floor as I try to collect myself.

I notice that we are not the only family up here. Another mom in a pool chair watches our exchange. This is not the time or place for hysterics. I clench and unclench my fists.

Maybe if I lean a little to the right, I can push John in the pool. Or what is the classic move? I throw a drink in his face. The thought brings back my smile. I look up.

"Stella, I am…we are glad you are okay," John speaks first, dropping his hand to his side when he realizes what he was doing.

I think back to the last time he touched me. When he leaned in for that quick peck on the cheek at our pool party. My heart thumps. John looks good. He is still handsome; that has not changed in the last eight days.

"Yes, it has been a crazy week," I exclaim and glare over at Rain. She looks a little embarrassed, but she tries to smile at me.

"Mom, this is Dad's friend, Rain, and her daughter, Dove. Rain helped us get home and to New York City. She speaks like five languages and knows so much stuff about the history of the world. She even got us a ride on a private plane. It was much nicer than the plane we rode over on the first time," Paul cuts into the awkwardness between the adults. This is the first time I am grateful that teenagers can be self-absorbed. I try to focus on getting through this. One moment at a time. My internal emotions are extreme. I feel like I am being shredded apart by John and yet I am jumping for joy on the inside at being reunited with Paul.

"Hello Rain, it is nice to meet you. Thank you for taking care of my son," I say as nicely as I can. I really want to punch her. I control myself, but barely.

I want to scream at John. I want to hug him, too. Until a few days ago, I would have said that I thought we were happily married. It is tearing me apart. Paul is standing next to me, and he does not understand that my heart is shattering like the ten million crystal pieces of the chandelier in the lobby below us.

I turn to John, "I found—I mean, we found your journal."

I turn to Jane and Chris who I suddenly recall are standing behind me, witnessing my joy and pain. I wave to them to join us.

"I spoke with General Patterns earlier today, in-person. He and his assistant, Captain Jones are working to clear your name and arrest Steve."

John nods his head. I can see John knows that I know about everything, and he is not hiding the truth…he is not hiding them.

"Yes, General Patterns called me about an hour ago letting me know my wife had been to see him. He said that you were one tough cookie." John looks at me with a smile. I try hard not to read into it. It is like he is proud of me. The fact that John refers to me as his wife rocks me.

It is like he is taking a knife to my heart. Again, I want to knock him in to the pool. Paul grabs my attention.

"Mom, you would not believe it. Dad fought the guys who kidnapped us. He used a gun he stole from the bad guys and a wooden table. It was better than a video game. He said he would teach me to fight like him. Then we ran through this town like we were in the Disney movie Aladdin from when I was a kid. There were in even camels in the street," he takes a breath and I can tell he is excited. "After that, we hopped a ride through the desert on the back of a pick-up truck. You should have seen it. It was so cool. It was like I was in an adventure movie. Mom did you know Dad speaks French?" Paul continues excitedly. It is like he is eight years old again. He is bursting with news. I move to hug him again.

"No, I did not know your dad spoke French. There are a lot of things about your dad that I did not know," I look at John and Rain pointedly. "It sounds like you had quite an adventure."

I take a deep breath.

Chapter 21

"John," I introduce them, "this is Agent Jane Phoenix and Agent Chris of the CIA," I realize I still do not know Chris's last name. "They have been conducting an investigation similar to yours. After our house burned down, we started to work together. They helped me find you, both." I squeeze Paul again in an awkward sideways hug.

Jane reaches her hand forward and shakes John's hand. She is interested in talking to him about his case. They step to the side. Chris steps forward to my side. I am now standing between Rain and Chris. Chris breaks the tension by speaking up first.

"Stella, why don't I show you to your hotel room?"

He rests his hand on my shoulder. I accept his touch because I am falling apart and could slide down to the ground at any minute. My bravado is slipping.

"Paul walk your mom downstairs and help me check in. How do you like the hotel?" I ask my son. My emotions are raw. I am trying to act normal for Paul's sake.

"Hey, Dad!" Paul shouts. "I am going to go down to our room with Mom to check-in." He misunderstood that I am going to a different room than them. My heart breaks a little more. I try to explain without going into details.

"Paul, I think it is best for now that I have some space of my own away from your dad, Rain, and Dove. It has been a long week for me," it is one of the hardest things I have ever had to say out loud.

John gives Paul the thumbs up sign. They seem to have gotten really close through this ordeal without me.

We pick a hotel towel up for Paul as we walk back towards the elevator with Chris. Rain has picked up Dove who is waving goodbye to Paul. Jane and John continue to talk. I can see they are having a very serious conversation. Jane does not look up as we leave. As the elevator door closes, Paul tells us more about his adventure with his dad. Chris puts his hand on my back in elevator. It is comforting. I allow myself to lean into him. I realize that John and I are going to need to talk without an audience. And very soon we are going to have to explain a few things about our new reality to Paul. Being an adult hurts.

Chris and Paul help me check-in and escort me to my new home-away-from-home, room 410. I watch Paul look at the city from my hotel window. He continues to convey details about flying out of Yemen on a private plane to Morocco, Fayetteville, and New York. He lets me know how private planes work, that they land at a separate part of the airport and sometimes even have their own building. Everyone on the staff is really nice, and they have food choices that are different for him and Dove. I am not really listening to the details. I cannot believe it's been over a week since I have seen him. All I can do is watch him afraid he is going to disappear. I cannot take my eyes off of Paul as he talks. I think he has grown another inch, and he definitely needs that hair-cut I thought about last Monday as he bounded up the steps towards me during our pool party.

Paul keeps talking about how he really liked the limo and driver that brought them to the hotel. He informs me that it was way better than a taxi. I think about how his life has changed and will continue to change since our pool party. We will never be the same.

I examine his new clothes and take in his new shoes. I reflect that I have probably bought every pair of shoes before these that Paul has ever worn. As he grew, we would go to the mall and find a department store clerk to measure his feet in the Brannock metal foot measuring device. Every new school year, it was a game to guess his new shoe size. My heart warms at the memory. Paul picked out his own tennis shoes from when he was toddler, always wanting something new with the flashing lights when he was small. Last year, he just had to have Michael Jordan's.

I think back to all the tennis shoes we have purchased over the years. Time is flying by, and I am lucky to have found Paul. I need to focus on the good. I realize that Paul is still talking, and I try to pay attention. My heart fills with joy.

Paul has transitioned to their trip to a Yankees game last night, and he explains that they sat behind the dugout. He was sure he was going to catch a foul ball. His dad had even bought him a new glove right in the stadium gift shop.

I move to stand next to him at the window. Paul's world is changing. All of our worlds, starting with the event eight days ago in the front yard to now, standing here in this hotel room on Fifth Avenue, are changed. We have been on a bullet train that altered the trajectory of our lives forever. We cannot go back to our little family unit in Fayetteville. Too much has happened. I watch Paul, and I know I am going to start to cry. I am going to break down. It is all overwhelming. I touch Paul's hair.

Chris catches me wrestling with my emotions.

"Hey Paul, why don't we give your mom a minute to freshen-up? I'll walk you back up to your dad," Chris suggests quietly.

I move in and give Paul another hug.

"Sure, okay. Mom, I'll see you in a few minutes, okay?" Paul hugs me back.

I can tell he is unsure about leaving my side. We all have a lot to work through. Chris touches my shoulder and leads Paul from the room. I sit down on the edge of the bed, slip off my flats, and start to cry big, messy tears as the hotel room door closes.

I stay there for few minutes, feeling sorry for myself and happy that my son is safe. I go into the bathroom to wash my face and fix my hair. There is a knock on my door.

I walk across the room; the carpet is soft on my bare feet. I open the door, and John is standing there. I swallow and step back. He is alone. John walks into the room. We stand less than two feet apart as the door closes behind him. We have been married for over sixteen years, but I do not know what to say or what to do now that we are alone. The last eight days have changed us.

Have changed me.

I step forward, and he wraps me in his arms and lays a kiss on my forehead. It feels normal and strange to be with him like this.

"Stella, thank you for going to General Patterns. I had not been able to get him on the phone before this afternoon. I had been trying the last few days. By the way, you look great. Have you lost weight?" he pauses. "I am glad you are here," John says close to my ear.

"You and Paul missing were some of the scariest days of my life," I whisper into his chest. Our old dynamic is coming alive. I can feel us slipping back into our roles.

John slides his hand up and down my back.

I start to cry. I cannot help it. The worry of the last week crashes over me. John reaches to wipe my tears; I feel his body; he is going to kiss me. *NO! Not after everything. NOT with Rain here.*

I slap him hard.

The sound echoes in the quiet of room.

I step back from his hands, away from his body.

I glare at John. He is such an asshole. I cannot believe what a total jerk he is…*have I lost weight?* rings in my head.

John rubs his face. Looking at me like he has never seen me before.

"I am sorry I hurt you. I should have handled this better," John says slowly. John moves in again trying to bridge the distance I have created.

"Yes, you should have told me the truth. You cheated on me," I quietly rail at him. "You ruined our marriage, our life …have you told Paul?" My tears have stopped, the last part comes out as a shriek. I want to smack him again.

John tries to pull me for a hug. I shake my head at him and move away from his hands.

How does he not realize everything has changed?

"No, John. I am angry and sad. We are over and getting a divorce. I don't even know how to talk to you. How could you? We had a home and family. I have supported you in your military career, in our life for over sixteen years," I hiss at him, backing away more.

"With Rain, it started out, she was a contact…I thought she was a way for me to gain information on the gun-running through her father's contacts. I never meant it to go so far," John tries to explain as he reaches to hold my hands. He sounds contrite. I do not care.

I shut him down.

I walk across the room to the window away from John, away from his touch. I have so many questions, but they really don't matter. This is the end of us. We are over. Our marriage is over. I close my eyes.

"John, you cannot have everything. That is not how this works. YOU do not get two families, two wives," I say with my back to him. I am shaking with anger.

Slow tears start to fall down my face. I do not wipe them away. Two families and only one will win. This is hard. I hate him, and I still love him.

When all the cards are on the table, everything I know now, I lose. I watch the traffic below as it rushes forward. Everything is moving too fast.

"What did you think? That you could have both families, that I would be okay with you and Rain? And Dove. When were you going to tell me you had a daughter? You have broken my heart," I cry out. "Do you even care?"

My hands are shaking. I feel John's indecision. He starts to move to take me in his arms, again, but I hold up my hand to stop him without looking at him. I know he is still my handsome husband. I am holding strong by a string here. There is a little part of me that still wants him, but I cannot let him use me. I must stay strong. I cannot let him wipe this away like it is nothing. I am not nothing.

John sits down in the one chair in the room by the desk. I hear him making soft sounds. I look back, and he is crying too. I watch him and my heart aches for our marriage, for the people we used to be. "Of course, I care. You are the mother of my son. We have been married for sixteen years. You have always been there for me whenever I needed you."

How can this be how we end? I am falling apart.

This is the first time I have seen John shed a tear. Maybe, he has finally realized all that he has thrown away. Somehow, I still want to comfort him. Old feelings are hard to dissolve, and I see him as my guy and all the things we have been though over the years. A week ago, I would have done almost anything for him, given John whatever he needed.

I cannot be there for John, now I must be there for me.

I wipe my face with my hand and take a deep breath. I can move forward from here. I do not need to turn this into a Real Housewives' drama with a broken-up hotel room to prove this marriage is over, as much as I want to throw a lamp at his head. I am strong enough to walk away from John and his duplicitous ways. I know that now, after everything that has happened to me this week.

I deserve better. I deserve someone who wants me; who cares about me.

"We need to sit down and explain this to Paul," I finally say. "He did not really understand why I need my own room at the hotel. He is used to us being a family unit together, and that will not be happening moving forward."

"Yeah, I guess I did not think this through. Any of it," John states. "I am sorry, Stella. I mean really sorry, dammit. You have been a good army wife. You put up with a lot over the years."

John's praises are not romantic declarations of love that touch my heart; they are only words, platitudes. He is not saying that he needs me or wants me.

I look out the window at the city, all the people, all the traffic, and even with my husband a few feet from me, I feel alone.

"Stella, you have to understand being undercover and meeting Rain, it was not planned. At first, she was part of the job. A way to get closer to the gun runners, but when Dove came into our lives all that changed. Dove is an amazing little girl."

Our marriage is crumbling before me into a pile of sand. I see it slipping away and there is nothing I can do to stop it. John's words hurt me. His actions, his relationship with Rain, his confession about Dove hammer into me. We cannot go back, and our new lives moving forward will be apart. It is like a tree that is split by lightning. One half has fallen into a river that is rushing away and the other is standing at the bank. There is no way to put the tree back together; it cannot live that way. The two parts no longer fit. One part will move on down the bank, maybe a seed will put down roots and start again. The other piece left on the bank will try to mend and grow strong on its own, knowing a piece of itself has moved on. I must be strong and move on from him.

John does not deserve me.

Eight days ago, I was worried we were not having enough sex and now we will never have sex again. Sometimes, life has a funny way of showing you how wrong you were about your problems…about people.

Maybe…eventually, I know I can forgive him, but not today. John and I have a lot of history. John made a terrible decision, but he has always been a good dad to Paul. I cannot let the anger in me fester, or I will be a mean and cranky woman, letting his betrayal tear me apart, hollowing me out. I take one last look at the lamp. It probably would have been fun to smash it.

I step towards John. I am not going to let his betrayal destroy me.

I am stronger than him.

"I am going to need some time to be angry with you. *You lied to me*, you cheated on me, and you betrayed our marriage," my anger is palpable in the room. "You screwed up, but for the good of our son, I am going to be as nice as I can. I will not say that I won't hate you, but I am going to move on with my life. I think that is best for both of us," my voice is almost a whisper in the room.

John looks at me, maybe…hopefully…he is realizing what he lost. "Stella, that is more than I deserve."

Well, at least we agree on that.

"John, we need to get a divorce quickly. I don't want to make a big deal about it." I take a deep breath.

"I think that is wise, I really do. You can have everything, whatever you need," John's voice is calm as he tries to reassure me.

This is all too real for me. Two adults dividing our life like leftovers at a picnic. I close my eyes. I need to get my bearings; the pain of John's easy acceptance is like another stab in the heart. I knew deep down that he was not going to fight for me, that he had Rain, but to hear his straightforward acceptance of the end of our marriage, of his losing me, makes me sink like a stone. He is willing to walk away from everything we have built for Rain. He is giving me everything, and yet I feel like I have nothing.

I take another deep breath. Each step forward pulls us further apart. I see the strings breaking that held us together.

John speaks, pulling me back into the room, out of my head. His words drive me back towards rage.

"By the way, I sent an old friend to check on you in D.C., he lives there, an old army buddy. I saw on my new laptop when you started using our accounts again. When you were shopping, I got an alert. I did not want to leave Paul alone." In his unspoken words, I hear that he did not want to leave Rain and Dove alone. I feel the knife of heartbreak slice deeper into my heart. "We had only just arrived in New York City and had met up with Rain and Dove. We had already told Paul we had tickets to the Yankee game, and he was excited to go having never been to a major league game before. I told him we would keep searching for you after the game, that we deserved a break." After everything he had been through, I wanted him to have some fun, to be kid. You understand...so, I had my friend track you to the stores and said you looked fine. You were purchasing some new clothes and out to eat at a restaurant. He mentioned he saw you holding hands with a blonde woman in the lobby of your hotel—he trails off.

I glare at John.

I want to shake him.

Again, the chaos of the last eight days has helped me see him.

John is a jerk! Concerned for his own happiness and ease of life before me.

I cannot believe he is implying I did something with Jane. I am hurt that he sent a friend to check on me when he was only in New York City, an easy trip to D.C. I was kidnapped and shot at by intruders in our home, but he is talking about my shopping habits. I want to scream. *How was I married to this man for sixteen years? He is a self-absorbed ass.*

I try not to yell. I am barely holding it together. He has no idea what I have been through. "John, that blonde woman is CIA Agent Jane Phoenix, who found me after I was kidnapped by a mobster wanting to find the guns that were supposedly in our home. In all of this chaos, the CIA has been there for me, protecting me, while you have been here playing house with Rain, your new daughter and our son. How could you think I was fine? I thought you and Paul were missing and our home had burned down? You are amazing. How did I not see what a jerk you are before?"

My anger is white hot now. I stomp my feet in front of him. I cannot control the frustration that is pouring out of me at his easy dismal of my person...of everything that happened to me. He is not even a little concerned.

"Jane took me back to the hotel because she thought we were being followed, which I guess it turns out we were, *by your friend.* Jane is the one who brought me here to you; you spoke to her by the pool. I cannot believe you. You are an ass!"

My blood is boiling. I pace the room. If I was a comic book superhero, I feel like sparks would be flying out of me right about now setting this hotel room ablaze. I do not think I have ever been this angry or this hurt.

I am near to exploding because of his accusation. John's lack of consideration for me is evident in his words. He sent his friend. He was not even worried about me...my heart hurts. It is like he continues to stab me with a dull blade. I cannot take it anymore. I am done!

I am livid at John, at how quickly he dumped me and turned on me.

It's like he is trying to shift some of the blame of his life with Rain around and make me culpable for his blowing up our marriage. I want to throw something at this head. I have to stop myself from marching over to the lamp on the nightstand. My fingers clench into fists. I try to calm down. I run my hands through my hair pulling it straight. I hate him. John is the biggest jerk. I feel like I was blinded by his good looks for so long, I missed the part where he is a huge self-absorbed jerk. I know it has been a long week for all of us, but I really want to hurt him.

I decide to shift gears, or I will start an argument that will go nowhere.

"I think we can all stay here for a few days since we have no home to go to at this point. However, Paul is to stay with me."

John thinks about that. He gets up from the chair and moves to stand next to me. I move closer to the window, away from him. I want no contact.

"Why don't I move you into a bigger room like he has, a suite closer to us. It won't be on the same floor we are staying, of course. Then you two can be together. I think it is a good idea for us all to take a moment without all the craziness. That is what Rain and I have been trying to offer Paul since we got back to the states."

I want to say something as he mentions Rain again. Now, I see how insensitive John can be. But I stay still. I need to think about Paul first. It is killing me to accept his suggestion.

I need him to stop talking.

My gut reaction is to say no. I want to object to being near Rain and Dove, to a bigger room, a suite from them. I want to shout. Instead, I breathe out. I am an adult.

I work hard not to overreact or be petty. I know to decline would be foolish. First and foremost, I need to focus on what is best for Paul. I am not a teenager breaking up with her boyfriend. I am a grown woman and mom who has been through a lot and who needs to restore a little bit of order in her life and Paul's life.

"You do not have any luggage?" John asks looking around.

"The house burned down, John," I state, annoyed with him. "I have had a pretty hard time the last eight days. Not that you asked what happened to me. I did tell you some of it. Obviously, you were not listening," I am snappy, it is not my job to explain things to John anymore.

Before we can leave there is a knock at the door. John goes to open it, ushering Jane into my room. "I am glad I found you both here alone. That makes this much easier for me."

"Jane, this really is not a good time. John and I are having a private discussion. Can this wait?" I implore my new friend.

"No, I am afraid this cannot wait, Stella. Steve is waiting for me. I need to take care of you two before Chris figures things out." Jane pulls out her gun, walking into the room.

I am confused by her words. *Why is Steve waiting for her?*

"Jane, what are you talking about? Steve is the criminal mastermind behind all of this. You were with me when we found John's journal. What are you doing?"

"What am I doing? I am choosing me for the first time. Don't you see the military chose the general and blew me up and then fixed me and sent me back out there to fight more bad guys? They did not care about me. *Steve* cares about me. We have a plan. He *loves me*. When you found the journal, I did not know what to do, but then when you went to take a shower in the hotel, I called Steve. We came up with a plan to be together and continue two pin this all on you two." John steps closer to Jane.

"Jane, you don't want to do this. Hand me the gun. You don't want to ruin your career," he implores her.

"Ha, my career…five years trying to find a gun-runner and nothing…do you think they give out awards for that? *no*. My career was going nowhere. Then I met Steve. He is brilliant. With his help I solve the case, the biggest case of my career and I get the guy! I win!" She laughs. She has this carefree, happy mood about her that I have not seen before. Jane is almost giddy with the excitement of her triumph.

"Jane, you don't want to hurt me. I helped you. Let's talk about this," I am pulling at any lose end I can find. I notice she is standing in front of the open bathroom door. I move slowly towards her.

"Yes, Stella you did. You ran off with Chris looking guilty. You gave me the bank account information that I took pictures of that day in the vault when I you thought I was just sitting there, so now you look even more guilty, and to top it off, you two are going to die together locked in a lover's embrace in a very expensive hotel room you could not afford on your military salary. You guys were greedy, greedy, greedy, blah blah blah the end of your story. I am going to tell General Patterns that John was the one who set Steve up with his phony little journal and with you two out of the way, it is going to be easy. John do you think I will finally get an award for solving this?" She waives her gun at John almost carelessly as her phone goes off.

She looks down. She has received a text message, "You see I had a choice, turn in Steve, the man I love, who loves me or get rid of you two and live happily ever after. I choose love," a sickly-sweet smile touches her face. "It's Steve. He is downstairs to join me. I need to go." She moves to answer him on her phone typing her reply. Involved in her lover's message, I take the opening.

I use my body weight to shove her back into the bathroom.

She slides onto the marble floor from the carpet falling backward. John goes to grab her gun as she fires a shot wildly.

Jane's phone clatters to the floor. The half-typed message to Steve wanting to be sent.

There is not room for all of us in the bathroom, and I stand there helplessly watching in the door frame.

Jane and John wrestle for her gun. It is as if it is happening before me in slow motion. "Steve," I hear her plead as John almost wrestles the gun from her hand.

Before it slips free, she fires again, this time hitting John in the side. He is pushed back and loses his grip on the gun.

I have no choice; I pick up the closet object to me, the lamp sitting next to the bathroom door that moments ago I wanted to throw at John, and I smash it into her face. I stare down the barrel of the gun she has aimed at me.

The lamp crashes onto the floor around her with a loud crack. The pieces scatter like a million puzzle pieces as the gun drops to the floor.

Without thinking, I pick up the gun and shoot, hitting Jane. John moves to stop me. Putting his hand over mine on the gun.

"Stella, she is dead you can stop now." I look at John. Blood covers his shirt. I realize I am crying. I wipe away my tears with my free hand.

My hand is shaking.

"Are you sure?" The words come out unsteadily.

John takes the gun from my hand and backs me away from the bathroom door closing it and leaving Jane inside on the floor.

I stand there shocked by what I have done. I killed Jane.

Chapter 22

Holding the gun, John falls into the chair by the desk. His hand is soaked in blood. My hands are still shaking as I reach for my phone in my back pocket to dial 911. I put it on speaker.

"John, I am calling for help. Hang in there." I grab the comforter off the bed and help him press it into his wound, hoping to stop the bleeding. "John, you are going to be okay, do you hear me? We got this."

"...911—What's your emergency?" breaks into the room.

"My husband, John, has been shot in the side. We need an ambulance to the Peninsula Hotel on Fifth Avenue, room *410*," I spill out.

"Are you okay, ma'am? Where is the shooter?" I point to the bathroom while talking on the phone. Realizing the person on the other end cannot see me I respond.

"The shooter...she is dead in the bathroom. Hurry, he is bleeding. There is a lot of blood."

"Ma'am, what is your name?"

"Stella Anne Finch. I am in room *410*. Please hurry." I am a mess of adrenaline and shock.

"Ma'am, please stay on the line with us," the operator responds.

"John, John stay with me. Are you okay?" I try to clean the blood off his arm with the side of the comforter.

"Stella...Jane...said...Steve...in...the building," John tries to tell me, but his words are low. It is hard to hear him. I figure out what John is trying to tell me, and I jump up.

"Crap, Chris. I need Chris. John, take my phone. Help is on the way."

I leave my phone with the speaker on next to John. I do not want to hang-up in case they need more information or cannot find us, I sprint for the door and out into the hallway, running for the elevator. I need to get to Chris. He is with the Paul at the pool. I press the elevator button a hundred times. Praying it will hurry. I jump into the elevator, pressing the button for the pool level with force. No one is in the elevator and, luckily, it does not stop. I watch it climb floors literally jumping up and down willing it to move faster. I am a bundle of nerves as I dash off the elevator searching for Chris and Paul. I see them standing with Rain on the far side of the Pool.

"Chris, Chris, I need you," I shout as I run towards them. I arrive and the words spill out of me.

"Colonel Steve Whitman is in the building. John has been shot. The ambulance is on its way. We need to go." They stare at me like I have grown two heads. I grab Paul's hand. "We need to go."

I start with Paul to elevator and Chris follows. Rain scoops up Dove and joins us in the elevator as the door is closing.

"Did you say that John has been shot?" she asks.

"Yes, I called the ambulance. They are on their way." I turn to Chris. "Steve Whitman is here in the building. Is there someone you can call for back-up?"

"Stella, where is Jane? I am texting the team for back-up now and she is not answering me. I have the CIA sending reinforcements to the hotel now." I see he has his phone out in his hand. Texts are coming through one after the other.

"Jane is dead. I shot her in our room. She was working with the colonel. She was trying to kill us." Chris looks as shocked as I feel as he absorbs my words. I pull Paul closer to me as we exit the elevator and head to my hotel room. I had left the door open in my haste.

Rain rushes in ahead of us and falls to the floor before John holding Dove between them. She is comforting him.

"John, I am here. Dove and I are here. It is going to be okay," her words come out through her tears. John grabs her hand and holds on. He is very weak. The ambulance is still on the way.

"Stella, I need to go to the lobby and direct the team and look for the colonel," Chris lets me know as he looks around my hotel room. "Where is Jane?"

I point to the closed bathroom door.

As he is about to leave, the paramedics arrive with hotel security and a police officer. As they enter the room, Chris shows him his badge and explains the situation.

"This is Stella, Paul, and John Finch and Rain and Dove. They are under the protection of the CIA. We have a body in the bathroom and this man," pointing to John, "needs attention. He has been shot," Chris turns to hotel security and the police officer. "We have a dangerous criminal in the building. Colonel Steve Whitman. We need to apprehend him before he is gone. I can send your people his picture. A team of CIA agents is on the way to lead this search."

I watch John and Rain together. They are a couple, whispering and holding hands.

I am in a state of disbelief over John and Rain's show of affection. After our conversation earlier in this room where John agreed to the divorce, I knew this relationship was a reality; however, seeing it in person is staggering. It is one thing to know your marriage is ended, that your husband has a lover and has moved on to someone else. It is another to see it before your eyes. The bombshell of seeing them like this is like a bolt of lightning to my heart.

I watch John and Rain for a moment, too stunned to move, before I notice that Paul is watching them too.

My mom radar kicks in, and I stop feeling sorry for myself.

"Paul, it looks like they are going to take your dad to the hospital. He is going to be okay. Your dad is a tough guy. Why don't we go to your room and collect your things? We can follow them to the hospital," I turn Paul away from his dad and Rain. "Paul, are you okay, buddy?" I probe, resting my hand on his shoulder.

"Yeah, are *you* okay, Mom?" he replies. He is still fixated on his dad and Rain. I can see events are starting to click in his head.

"Yes, I think I am going to be okay. Eventually. Your dad and I talked. Things are going to be changing for us all," I tell him, hugging him to my side. Chris walks over to us from the emergency team.

"Stella, I need to go down to the lobby and meet my team. Are you going to be okay here?"

"Actually, would you mind escorting us up to Paul's room? I want to get him in some dry clothes before we head to the hospital to be with his dad. Besides we do not even know if Colonel Steve is even in the building or not. He is probably long gone."

Chris looks at me for a minute and makes the decision to help me. It will only take a second for Paul to change out of these wet swim shorts and grab a clean T-shirt.

As the team of paramedics lifts John onto a gurney, I move past Rain to speak with John who seems to be doing better. His eyes are open, and they have stopped the bleeding.

"John, Paul and I will meet you at the hospital." I turn to the paramedics, "I am his wife; my son and I will meet you at the hospital. Which hospital are you taking him to?"

The paramedic looks from Rain to me and back again. "We are taking him to New York Presbyterian Hospital," she replies.

I am sure she has seen weirder things in New York City than a man shot with his girlfriend and wife in the room.

Rain, holding Dove, follows the paramedics out of the room. As she leaves, she hands Paul a room key. Hotel security is standing with the police officer waiting for us to leave the room. Chris has explained to them that Jane's body is in the bathroom, and I want to get Paul out of the room before they open the door. Chris lets them know he will be back as we head out to Paul's room. Jane's body and any investigation will fall under the purview of the CIA.

Chris is on his phone as we walk to the elevator. His team of CIA agents has arrived in the lobby to help scout for Colonel Whitman. So far there is no sign of him.

I am keeping Paul close as we take the elevator to his room. We enter his room and he scoops up his clothes quickly. He goes to the bathroom to change out of his wet swim shorts.

"You shot Jane?" he asks quietly.

"Yes, she was going to kill John and me. She was working with Colonel Steve Whitman. They had set-up…going to continue with the set-up story on John. She was crazy…crazy in love, I guess. Her and John struggled for the gun, John was shot, and I got it and I shot her. It happened very quickly," I try to explain, but it sounds farfetched even to me. Chris wants to ask more, but Paul comes out of the bathroom in new dry clothes, and we head back to the elevator. Once again, we were all alone in the elevator going to down the lobby. Chris scrolls through his text messages from the CIA team there is no sign of Colonel Steve. I see Chris has sent the team a picture of the colonel in his uniform, it must be his official military photo.

Stepping out into the lobby, I falter. Standing there, not three feet away from me, is Colonel Steve Whitman. He looks like a normal, everyday tourist in casual pants and a Hawaiian shirt waiting for his wife or a business associate. I almost cannot believe it is him, he has colored his hair to a blonde from the salt and pepper gray it was before, but then I spot his big gold Rolex watch on his wrist.

I need to protect Paul.

Instinctively, I grab Paul's wrist and pull him behind me. At the same time, I step closer to Chris. We stop walking, and I can tell Chris has seen him too. We are on the same page. Colonel Steve Whitman is standing right before us with his back to us. He is standing next to a large pillar. I motion for Paul to hold back, and he move towards the wall away from me. Chris takes out his gun as the colonel turns around, seeing us. I realize too late that I am in the middle between Chris and Steve. In my nervousness, I shout a greeting at him, "Hi, Colonel Steve," hoping that other agents nearby in the lobby will hear me.

"*You*, but *you*," the colonel sputters at me.

"Are supposed to be dead…let me finish that sentence for you, Colonel." I cannot help it; it feels good to see the confusion and pain on his face as he realizes his plan has finally fallen apart.

Steve growls at me, pointing his finger. "I worked hard on that pretty blonde CIA agent to help me. All I really wanted her to do is have you ended. I had it all figured out. I could retire from the army with an award for ferreting out John's corruption. It would have been a feather in my cap, maybe even a presidential medal," Steve spits out, his eyes look wild. Steve is a man on the verge of falling apart.

His words are crazy.

Steve removes a gun from behind his back and points it at me. It is the second time today I have had a gun pointed at me, and I do not like the feeling. I realize the agents behind Steve do not know that he is armed.

"Colonel, why don't you put that gun down and we can talk about how you can still get that presidential medal. I mean, you must know John is not really my favorite person these days," I stall for time. The agent behind Steve motions to Chris. I realize they have a plan in motion.

"Colonel Steve, maybe we could work out a deal you and me," I say in a flirty voice. His eyes light up as the CIA agent behind him knocks him over the head with his gun. The colonel crumples to the floor, and Chris picks up his gun securing it. Paul runs over to me.

"Mom, you played that so cool. That was awesome." I hug Paul tightly, happy that Colonel Steve is no longer going to be a problem in our life.

"Stella, I need to stay here and get Colonel Steve, Jane, and the case wrapped up. Is it okay if I put you in a car with a driver to the hospital? I think you are going to be okay now," Chris says to me as I release Paul.

Chris walks us through the lobby full of normal people who have not had chaos enter their lives. I see moms ignoring their children as they answer messages on their phones. Business people rushing to their next big deal not worrying about their family. Before we get in the car, Chris reaches for my hand. "Stella, what you did back there was pretty crazy, but it worked. Next time, maybe remember I am here to save you," he says with a little laugh. "Next time, I think I am done with all of this chaos for a while." I smile back at him. "Hey, Stella, when things calm down a bit around here would you like to go out to for a drink or maybe have dinner with me?" Chris actually looks a bit nervous and shy has he asks.

I don't have to think about my response, "Yes, I would like that." I lean in and give Chris a hug.

I step back as our car pulls up. "Paul, take care of your mom she has had a rough week."

He says touching Paul shoulder. Paul looks at me and smiles.

"We had better go and check on John," I say as Paul slides into the back seat of the sedan.

Chris seems reluctant to let go of my hand. "Take care of yourself, Stella." He reaches up and smoothes down a piece of my hair that had flown in my face.

"I will, you too, Chris." I can tell he sees me, really sees me as a woman and that gives me a little thrill as our hands release. I look over to the lobby and the line of police cars before sliding into the car beside Paul. Chris shuts the door behind me, and I wave goodbye.

This is a new day, and I am not going to take anything for granted. I am leaving all of this chaos behind me and starting anew. We, Paul and I have come out of all the crazy of the last week to the other side. I am grateful to have my son back. I reach over and hug Paul to me. Sitting back against the sit

I look forward, and smile I relax for the first time in eight days, knowing we are safe. We are going to be okay. I am going to be okay.